Adventures
of a VIP

Adventures of a VIP

...

Vivian McDermott

ISBN: 0997055316
ISBN 13: 9780997055313
Library of Congress Control Number: 2016904646
CreateSpace Independent Publishing Platform
North Charleston, South Carolina

Author's Note

• • •

THIS IS A WORK OF fiction in which I have drawn on many of my own experiences as a visually impaired person. Like the main character in this story, I have a degenerative eye disease called Retinitis Pigmentosa. Regardless of their individual characteristics, by their very nature, degenerative diseases curtail activities and shape lives, sometimes messing with minds in the process.

This is not a memoir – because memoirs have to be true. If you think you recognize any of the characters or events described in these pages, remember that they may be based on fact, but details have been embellished, augmented, omitted or completely fabricated, and names have been changed to protect both the innocent and the guilty.

Aknowledements

• • •

My journey as a writer began when I was ten years old and my grandma, Mazelle Robinson, taught me to write letters. Several years later when those letters amused her and the friends with whom she shared them, she planted the idea in my mind that someday, I should write a book.

The idea that I could become a published author was re-awakened when my high school friend and co-author Sheralynn Ries convinced me that together, we were capable of writing and publishing a book that other people would read and enjoy. (The Crone's List – December 2015)

Every writer needs someone in their corner – a coach of sorts. My coach is Jacque Verrall. We have been friends since we were ten years old, supporting and encouraging each other throughout the many phases of our lives. When it comes to writing, I depend on her for encouragement, honest feedback, reader insights and editing.

Last, but not least, as the saying goes--kudos to my friends and my entire family, especially my husband. Whether you teased me about being a world famous author, previewed the book, talked about the book to friends and acquaintances, or just said "well done" – your support and encouragement are greatly appreciated.

CHAPTER 1

Diagnosis

• • •

DIANA TOOK A DEEP BREATH and made a conscious effort to stop tapping her foot, realizing at the same time that she was also drumming her fingers on the arm of the chair. Obviously she was nervous, and she tended to fidget when she got nervous.

For the past two hours, she had been moving up and down the hallway of this clinic, in and out of one exam room after another. Although she had lost track of how many rooms she'd been in, she knew that there were four different technicians, all of them women dressed in identical white lab coats. One was tall and thin with her thick blond hair pulled into a ponytail at the nape of her neck and a pair of gold wire rimmed glasses perched on her nose. One was short and slender with sleek black hair styled in a wedge shaped bob that was short in the back and fell just below her chin in the front. She was the only one without glasses. Diana wondered if she wore contacts instead. The third one was short and round with tight gray curls and silver framed glasses dangling from a matching silver chain around her neck. The last one had shoulder length dark curly hair held back on either side of her face with matching gold clips. She wore glasses with over-large square frames in a shade of sparkly hot pink that was nearly neon. They were so bright that they practically glowed on her face, and just looking at them made Diana smile.

Each technician cleaned the diagnostic machine with antiseptic wipes while explaining the next test. All of them were generous with eye drops before they told her to look left, look right, close one eye, open both eyes, read the letters, focus on the pinwheel, or push a button when the light flashed. Some of them administered more than one test before handing her off to the next person.

There were quite a few tests, and Diana was pretty sure she hadn't scored very well on a couple of them, like the one where she was supposed to look straight ahead and push a button whenever a light flashed. It was hard to judge how long the test took, but it was easy to count how many times she pushed the button. She wouldn't have thought to keep track, but she only pushed the button twice for the test on her right eye, so she paid attention when they tested her left eye, and she only pushed the button eight times. That couldn't be good. She had that same sick feeling in the pit of the stomach that she used to get back when she was in school and hadn't studied for a test. She knew these were not the kinds of tests one could study for, but even so, she hated performing poorly. Now, with a pounding headache and bleary eyes, she waited in yet another exam room to see the doctor himself.

Dr. Letz was the ophthalmologist whose name was on the door of this prestigious Seattle eye clinic. He had come very highly recommended, and Diana was both curious to meet him and apprehensive about what he would have to say. She had known something was wrong with her vision for most of her life, or at least since she was ten years old and had to get corrective lenses. Since then she had gone for routine eye exams and updated the prescription for her glasses when needed. That had helped, but it hadn't entirely solved the problem. Sometimes she just didn't see very well. More specifically, she didn't see things that everyone else was easily able to see. As she waited for Dr. Letz, she worried that this exam would either be another waste of time and money without giving her an answer, or that the answer would not be good news. Briefly, she wished she hadn't come, yet even as the thought skittered through her head, she scolded herself for her cowardice. The first step in solving a problem was identifying what it was. Of course she wanted answers.

She straightened as the door opened and Dr. Letz entered the room. She judged him to be about five feet ten, the same height as her husband. Her eyes were too bleary to see much more than that he was slender, had silver hair, and wore wire rimmed glasses and a white lab coat. He placed her chart on the counter that ran the length of the wall. Briskly, he introduced himself, washed his hands, reached for the eye drops and handed her a tissue. He wasn't rushed exactly, but he was definitely efficient, Diana thought. She tilted her head for another round of eye drops, this time from two different bottles, one designed to numb and the other to dilate.

Dr. Letz dimmed the lights, throwing the room into semi-darkness and directed her to lean her forehead against the bar and place her chin on the little ledge. Apparently, she thought as she complied, someone else wiped down this machine between patients. She curled her fingers into fists in her lap as he shined bright lights into her eyes and gave her instructions to look straight ahead, left, right, up and down. The exam took only a minute or two, but it seemed like much longer. The bright exam lights always made her feel as if sharp needles were poking into her eyeballs. Her head pounded and her stomach churned as she fought to keep her eyelids from slamming shut. She'd never heard anyone else complain about an eye exam being painful, and that made her feel like a wimp.

At last, he doused the exam light, pushed the machine aside, and turned the overhead light back on. While Diana focused on breathing slowly and unclenching her fists, Dr. Letz sat down on a rolling stool that he pulled from under the counter, picked up a pen and made a few notes on her chart. When he had finished writing, he turned to face her.

"I have good news and bad news."

"Okay." Diana said, cautiously, mentally bracing herself. "Tell me the bad news first."

"The bad news is that you have Retinitis Pigmentosa." He paused, "Have you ever heard of it?" She shook her head.

"No."

"No reason why you would have." He assured her and then explained. "RP is a somewhat rare degenerative eye disease. By somewhat rare, I mean that about one in four thousand people have it. The condition is characterized by night blindness, narrowing peripheral vision, color blindness, and holes or gaps in the vision field." He paused as if inviting her to comment.

"I haven't noticed color blindness, and I'm not quite sure what you mean by holes in the vision field." Diana said, mentally sorting the symptoms he had listed and comparing them to her experiences, including the test with the flashing lights that she apparently hadn't seen. She had already figured out that one measured peripheral vision. "I definitely have night blindness, and narrowing peripheral vision."

"Think of your vision field as being made up of pixels something like a digital photograph," Dr. Letz explained. "And some of your pixels are missing." Diana considered his description and nodded.

"Okay." She said. "But I don't see those gaps?"

"In layman's terms, your brain fills in the missing pixels according to the background of whatever you are looking at." Dr. Letz replied.

"Ah!" Diana exclaimed, immediately grasping the concept. "And that's why I see blue sky but not the birds or planes everyone else can see?"

"That's right. As soon as some part of whatever you can't see moves out of the gap and into the functioning part of your vision field, then your brain will fill in the rest. Otherwise that item is invisible to you."

"That explains a lot!" Diana commented, thinking of her struggle to find things if she dropped them or laid them down somewhere, her tendency to become disoriented in new places, and her inability to

recognize the faces of new acquaintances. She pulled her attention back to Dr. Letz who was asking her a question.

"When did your first symptoms appear?"

"I was sixteen."

"You seem very definite about that." Dr. Letz raised an eyebrow.

"I had a car accident. Everyone thought I ran a stop sign, but I didn't. I never saw the other car coming, even though I distinctly remember carefully looking both ways, twice." She shrugged. "Gaps in my vision field would explain that, at least to me." Dr. Letz nodded and made a note on her chart. Then he looked up and continued.

"RP is hereditary, with symptoms usually beginning in the late teens or early twenties and getting progressively worse. There is no cure." Dr. Letz stopped speaking and waited patiently for her to absorb his words.

"Hereditary." Diana repeated, softly. She realized that his super-efficient persona had vanished and he seemed intent on making sure that she understood his explanations of her condition, like a teacher.

"Do you have children?" He asked, and Diana nodded.

"How old are they?"

"My youngest is twenty-six and my oldest is thirty-two."

"Boys or girls?" She wondered why it mattered as she told him that she had sons.

"Have any of them exhibited any symptoms similar to yours?"

"No."

"So they are past the usual age when symptoms begin." Dr. Letz nodded and made another note on her chart. "That's good news."

"Yes." Diana agreed. She felt as if she'd had a narrow escape without being aware of any risk. She had a severe eye infection when she was ten years old and then had to get glasses. Whether it was cause and effect or just an association of events, she always linked the onset of her vision problems with that infection. The thought that her eye problems might be hereditary had never crossed her mind, so she had not worried

about the eyesight of her children, at least not beyond making sure they got regular eye exams.

"Most people who have RP are legally blind by the time they are in their thirties. How old are you?"

"Fifty-six." Diana replied automatically as her mind caught on the phrase 'legally blind', and then her comprehension caught up with her hearing, and every nerve in her body went on full alert. Wait a minute! She was twenty years past her thirties, and she could still see. Sure, she had some problems with her vision; that was the reason she was here. But she could still see.

"That's the good news." Dr. Letz said. "You are fifty-six, and your straight-ahead vision, at least, is still pretty good." Dr. Letz cocked his head to one side before he continued.

"To be completely candid with you, I have never actually seen a case like yours, not in all my years of practice." Dr. Letz paused again, seeming to search for the right words. "Your particular symptoms do not fall within the usual parameters, so I have no hard data to go by. However, your vision appears to be deteriorating at a much slower rate than usual for someone with RP."

"But it will continue to get worse?" Diana asked.

"That's the nature of a degenerative disease, so yes; your vision will continue to get worse. But if the deterioration continues to go as slowly as it has so far, you will probably not go completely blind."

"Probably not." Diana repeated, somewhat dazedly. All her life she had been cursed with the ability to automatically imagine the worst case scenario for any situation. At that moment as if she were seated in front of a movie screen, she pictured herself trying to choose between a Seeing Eye dog and a white cane. With an effort, she turned the movie off and pulled her attention back to Dr. Letz.

"That's my best guess." She found this statement more than a little disconcerting. Doctors are supposed to be scientific, and he was guessing? She didn't know what to say, so remained quiet. Dr. Letz shrugged.

"It is an educated guess, if you don't mind my saying so, and it's the best I can do with the data I have, but it is still a guess." He gave her a penetrating look. "The testing we did today has established a base line. I would recommend that you monitor your vision with regular checkups so you can be aware of any changes."

"I've had regular eye exams since I was a child. I wonder why nobody picked up on this before now." Diana found her voice at last, her comment a thinly veiled question. Dr. Letz understood and answered promptly.

"Your symptoms are quite unusual, and probably too vague. To diagnose RP in the early stages, you have to be looking for it. There is no doubt that you have it, but as I said, you have a very mild case." He paused and repeated, "A very mild case."

"Is there anything I can do to help preserve the vision I have left?" Diana asked.

"Nothing that has been scientifically proven," Dr. Letz replied, again seeming to choose his words with great care. "Some people take supplements to support healthy eye function, like Bilberry, Lutein, and Vitamin A, to name a few."

"I've been taking supplements, including those, for years." Diana said ruefully, "I'm not sure it has helped."

"But you aren't blind, are you?" Dr. Letz asked pointedly, his eyebrows raised and one corner of his mouth quirked upwards into a smile.

CHAPTER 2

Forty Years Earlier

• • •

Sixteen year old Diana Williams had done babysitting to earn her own spending money since she was eleven, and while she adored kids, babysitting was a very sporadic way to earn money. Diana had a desperate need to earn money so she could purchase essential items like make-up, hair products, clothes and shoes. This house cleaning job, a couple of hours after school three days a week and sometimes a few hours on Saturday, was a much more reliable source of income. Nora had a large house, a toddler, and together with her husband, owned a business downtown. Diana liked working for her because she always left detailed written instructions for what she wanted done. Some days Diana cleaned the kitchen or the bathrooms, and other days she scrubbed floors or vacuumed the carpets, but today she had worked her way through a basket of ironing, while listening to music on the stereo. Now she was behind the wheel of the family station wagon on her way home.

Diana had been driving for over a year, which was common in Montana, where teens who took driver's education could get their driver's license as soon as they were fifteen. Conrad, Montana was a place where the farm kids, at least, had all been driving for years before they were old enough to take driver's training. They drove pickups, tractors, and grain trucks, sometimes even before they were old enough to start school. Diana couldn't personally imagine a five year old driving,

but she had heard stories from her friends at school and believed that it happened.

Diana's family lived in the country, so she was a country kid, but she wasn't a farm kid, and on the first day of driver's education, she was convinced that she was the only student in the class without previous driving experience. She felt clumsy and stupid sitting behind the wheel of the driver's education car for the first time, because, well, it really was her first time in the driver's seat. In spite of her angst, she managed to pass the course. Then she had to wait three weeks for her fifteenth birthday. She aced the written part of the driver's test, and on her second attempt, passed the driving part of the test too. It was a fluke when she managed to successfully parallel park her dad's station wagon. It felt like a tank compared to the driver's education car, which she also had trouble parking. But lucky or not, she had fulfilled the requirements so she had her picture taken and got her temporary license to use while she waited for the plastic one to arrive in the mail.

Diana's dad had been thrilled to have another driver in the family. The previous year, he had purchased and fixed up a used jeep for himself so they would have another vehicle in addition to the nine year old station wagon that served as their family car. As soon as she got her license, Diana became responsible for running household errands and driving to and from her own after-school job. Responsibility was not new to her; she also did the laundry, the housework and most of the cooking. Though she drove several times each week, Diana never felt entirely comfortable behind the wheel, and was a very cautious driver.

It was dusk on a dreary February day and starting to snow again, the flakes drifting lazily down from the sky. The snowfall from the previous week had been plowed and shoveled into piles that graced the sides of streets and driveways. Everything looked gray in the waning light under low hanging clouds, as she eased her dad's faded turquoise blue 1959 Chevy station wagon to a stop at the corner where Main Street intersected with 7th Avenue. She used her blinker to signal for a left turn and reminded herself that the streets were probably icy. There was no oncoming traffic when she looked left and right, and then looked again in each direction to make sure nobody was coming before she pressed gently on the accelerator and started into her turn. The jolt to the passenger side of the car came at the same time she heard the screech of grinding metal. The impact from the collision sent the station wagon skidding sideways until it stopped abruptly as the tires bumped hard against the curb on the opposite side of the street. Dazed, she sat with her fingers frozen around the steering wheel, her breath choppy and her heart thumping against her ribs.

People appeared at once to see if she was injured, and within minutes the sheriff's deputy rolled up in his police cruiser. She pried her fingers from the steering wheel and located the insurance and registration papers in the glove box, then retrieved her license from her purse which had fallen off the passenger seat spilling its contents onto the floor. She was glad they had gone over what to do in case of an accident as part of driver's education and that her dad had made sure she knew where the important papers were in the glove box. She handed everything to the deputy through the window when he approached her car.

"I need to call my dad." She said. The deputy was writing on a clipboard, but he paused and glanced at her.

"Okay, but then come right back to your car." She said she would. The nearest pay phone was on the other side of the street, right outside the door to the grocery store. She got out of the car and stood there for a minute to make sure her knees wouldn't buckle, and then walked across the street and the parking lot to the phone. It took three tries for her shaking fingers to insert the dime into the slot, and then she dialed the phone number for the newspaper where her dad worked.

"Dad, nobody is hurt, but I had a wreck." She said in a shaky voice when she reached him. She told him where she was and he came at once as she had known he would, because he was the kind of dad you could count on. He asked her to tell him what had happened, but not until later, when they were at home. She explained everything as she remembered it and he listened to her account of the accident. He didn't yell or lecture.

The following week, Diana and her dad sat side by side in front of the justice of the peace who leafed through the papers on his desk before he looked up and spoke.

"You've been cited for failure to yield causing an accident. Do you understand?"

"Yes." Diana replied.

"Do you have any questions or comments?" the judge asked, peering over his glasses at her. He had bushy eyebrows and a fringe of gray hair around his mostly bald head.

"No." She thought it would be pointless to comment. Although she was convinced the other driver had been speeding as he entered the city limits, he'd had the right of way, and she'd had the stop sign. At the scene of the accident, the deputy had been quite sure that Diana had not come to a complete stop at that stop sign. He hadn't said that, exactly, but his attitude conveyed his opinion that she was yet another careless teen-aged driver. She had not argued with him, had not commented at all in fact, and she wasn't going to say anything to the judge, either. She had already gone over and over the sequence of events in her mind without arriving at an answer to the question of why she hadn't seen the other car. She knew she had stopped. She distinctly remembered looking twice in both directions for oncoming traffic. Eventually she tired of replaying the accident on the television screen of her mind like an endless re-run, and decided that she must have been careless. The only thing she could do, really, was resolve to be more careful.

"I'm going to give you a choice of a thirty dollar fine or forfeiting your driver's license for thirty days." The judge said.

Diana had already thought about the possibilities and decided that she would rather lose her license temporarily than pay a fine. She didn't want to waste her hard-earned money on a traffic ticket because she was saving for a new pair of shoes. Most of her peers loved to drive and she had never admitted to anyone that she wasn't that crazy about it. Of course she was upset about the accident, but she was also a little bit relieved that she would have a month off from driving. She didn't mind riding the bus, and she knew that she could count on her friends if she really needed a ride somewhere other than to and from school.

Duane made no audible comment, but he did indulge in a mental groan when Diana told the judge she would forfeit her license for thirty days. He knew that the penalty she chose would cost him time and trouble, because the responsibility for running household errands and transporting his two younger daughters to and from their activities, which Diana had taken over last summer when she got her license, would temporarily revert back to him. When the paperwork was taken care of, Duane dropped Diana off at school and drove to work – lately that was the one place in his life where he was reasonably sure he knew what he was doing.

Duane was just under six feet tall, slender with dark hair and blue eyes. He was by nature a man of few words, but when it came to dealing with his daughters, he nearly always found himself not knowing what to say. His wife had died when the girls were small, and he was often overwhelmed by some of the unexpected aspects of parenting. He understood working hard and he had both a full-time and a part-time job in order to provide for food, shelter and clothing. He and his daughters disagreed on clothing, since he didn't really understand the need for the multiple pairs of shoes they insisted were totally necessary. As a kid, he had always worked for what he wanted and thought his girls should do the same, so he was proud that Diana was willing to work for the extra things she wanted. He encouraged all of his daughters to do the right thing and stay out of trouble, and he was willing to help them handle the physical details of whatever the latest crisis was, but he left them to sort through the emotional fallout on their own.

Duane was immensely relieved that nobody had been hurt in Diana's accident, and he didn't mind handling the insurance paperwork and the car repairs. Truthfully, a minor traffic accident was a ripple in his world when compared to dealing with some of the other things his girls did, especially Diana. She was the oldest, so he supposed the younger girls would follow in her footsteps, and he wondered if he would get any better at this parenting thing.

He had not known what to say or do when Diana started wearing make-up, so he had said nothing. He thought some of her skirts were more mini than skirt, but he didn't say anything about that either. He did feel obligated to ask her about missing school when one of her sisters mentioned that she'd stayed home, but then didn't know whether to be embarrassed, relieved, or worried when she told him she had cramps. When he had broached the subject of a curfew, Diana had told him in no uncertain terms that being responsible for household chores and cooking entitled her to more freedom in her personal life than a girl her age would normally be allowed, and how could he argue with that? He was a fair man, and when she put it that way, he thought she was probably right. Several months ago she had started dating, and he still shuddered at that memory!

He'd been working on his jeep in the garage one Saturday afternoon when Diana appeared at his elbow with a young man she introduced as Jim somebody. After the handshake he'd been at a loss, and the two of them might still be standing there staring at each other, but the kid asked him a couple of questions about his jeep. Duane wasn't much for small talk, but he didn't mind talking about cars, and the kid seemed to know a thing or two about engines. He was just starting to relax when Diana spoke.

"Jim asked me to go to the Lovin' Spoonful concert in Great Falls tonight. We should be back a little after midnight, okay?" He thought he stood frozen in place as he stared at her, but maybe he nodded because she gave a little wave and the next thing he knew, they were leaving.

He wanted to rush after them and make Diana stay home. That's what he wanted to do, but he didn't do it, mostly because he hadn't forgotten his first date with Diana's mother – and she had been fifteen.

• • •

"I knew this was a bad idea!" Diana muttered.

"Oh stop whining and just admit it was fun!" Kay replied.

"I'm freezing and I can't find my clothes." Diana said crossly. "That's not my idea of fun!"

"Here you go." Lynn giggled as she handed Diana her jeans, t-shirt and sandals. "Skinny dipping is a little chilly this time of year."

"Brilliant deduction! I believe I pointed that out already! In fact, I distinctly remember voting against the whole skinny dipping idea." Diana muttered as she hurried to get dressed, her teeth chattering.

At eleven p.m. towards the end of May, the water was cool and refreshing, and they felt quite daring when they stripped down to their underwear and waded out into the waters of Lake Francis until they were submerged to their necks. When they emerged from the water, though, the night air which had felt balmy when they were dry, chilled their wet skin.

"Let the record show," Kay reminded them as they finished dressing, "That I was out-voted. I wanted to go skinny-dipping, so we could say we'd done it, but the two of you refused to get naked!"

"Now you know how I feel – I'm always outvoted – and please do not tell me that this didn't count as skinny dipping!" Diana groaned.

"Technically, its underwear dipping but I guess we can still count it." Kay replied grudgingly.

"Underwear dipping, huh? Maybe we've created a new fad!" Lynn snickered.

"We'd have to tell people about it to start a fad. Count me out on that!" Diana said firmly.

"If we'd gotten naked, our underwear would still be dry, though. I wish I'd thought of that sooner, I would have voted the other way." Lynn shared a spirit of adventure with Kay. When she wasn't enthusiastically supporting Kay's ideas, she was thinking up ideas of her own.

"Too late now!" Kay retorted. "Hey! Where are you going?"

"To the car." Diana snapped. Kay reached out and caught Diana's arm pulling her more to the left.

"The car is this way, remember?" She said, linking arms and leading Diana towards the parking area. Remembering had nothing to do with it, Diana thought. She was totally disoriented and unable to see much of anything in the darkness. Idly, she wondered if her grandmother had been right that eating carrots would improve her eyesight. She'd never really liked carrots very much, and anyway, she thought it was probably already too late.

• • •

Diana, Kay and Lynn met during their sophomore year at Conrad High School. Lynn was a country kid who had attended school in Conrad since Kindergarten. Kay had gone to country school through the eighth grade, becoming a CHS student as a freshman. Diana had moved to Conrad from another state in the middle of her freshman year. Except that they were all oldest children who lived out of town, they didn't seem to have much in common. Perhaps it was their differences more than their similarities that sealed their friendship.

Kay, whose hazel eyes missed nothing, was artistic, smart, self-confident and outspoken. She was a pretty girl with delicate features, a peaches and cream complexion, and naturally curly auburn hair that brushed her shoulders. She ignored peer pressure and made her own choices in activities, clothing, and opinions. Her parents bought her a used car when she turned seventeen so she could drive to and from school and her other activities. It was convenient for them and opened up a whole new realm of possibilities for Kay and her friends.

Lynn was ambitious, articulate, intelligent and organized. Her chin length brown hair had natural golden highlights from spending summer days in the sun, and her brown eyes always seemed to be twinkling with humor and mischief. She made her own clothes, cut her own hair, excelled in school, and earned her spending money from several part-time jobs. She worked hard, played harder, and was always ready to do something fun. While her parents farmed the acreage her grandparents had homesteaded; she dreamed of moving on to the bright lights and excitement of life in the city.

Diana had blue eyes and brown hair that she usually tied back into a pony tail. She did not like to call attention to herself in any way, and was usually so quiet that the casual observer had no clue about her quick wit or her gift for sarcasm. At least once a week, for no real reason except that she didn't want to go, she skipped school. Even when physically present at school, she often made a mental escape by tucking a library book inside her text book so that she appeared to be studying while she was actually in the middle of an imaginary adventure. She tried, and usually failed, to be the voice of caution when her two friends embarked on a real adventure, but she always went along rather than be left behind.

Kay was engaged to be married right after their high school graduation, and she seemed to have a mental list of crazy things she wanted to do before she settled down. Diana could not imagine that anything, including marriage, would settle Kay down. Lynn was going to college after graduation, and knew that she would have to work to afford the cost. Maybe that's why she had gone along with all of Kay's ideas and come up with a few of her own. Diana hadn't decided what she would do after graduation, but she knew their friendship would change when they went their separate ways after high school. Maybe that's why she let them talk her into their crazy schemes.

• • •

One night, the three girls sneaked out after midnight to go for a ride in Kay's car. They couldn't be seen in town because it was after curfew, so they drove to Shelby and back and then they had to sneak back into their houses. Kay had prepared a schedule with what time she would be there to get them and she had even had them synchronize their watches.

Lynn's room was on the second floor of her family's farm house. She had removed the screen, climbed out her bedroom window, pulled the window back down leaving just enough room to slide her fingers underneath to push it up again when she returned, and replaced the screen. Then she tiptoed across the porch roof and climbed down a big cottonwood tree that grew so close to the house that her dad had been talking about cutting it down. Once on the ground, she slipped through the trees that surrounded the house and made her way to the road where Kay and Diana were waiting to pick her up.

The tough part was climbing up that tree to get to the roof of the porch so she could get back into her room. Lynn had been a little nervous wondering if she could do it. If Diana had been in her shoes, she wouldn't have tried, but Lynn was more daring. Her two younger brothers planned to build a tree-house in that tree over the summer. They had nailed pieces of wood to the trunk to form footholds and tied a rope around one of the branches to hang on to while climbing. Those two kids went up and down that tree like little monkeys all summer, even though they never did get around to building the tree house. Lynn planned to use their rope and footholds to get back into her room.

"Wish me luck!" Lynn said with a grin as she slipped out of the car that Kay had parked on the road and melted into the trees. Kay muttered a play by play as she followed Lynn's progress through the shadows and up the tree. Diana who lost sight of Lynn as soon as she got into the trees, held her breath listening to Kay's progress report and only relaxed when she saw the light go on in Lynn's upstairs room.

Diana's dad had his room in the basement on the far side of the house, leaving the two upstairs bedrooms for Diana and her younger sisters. She had tiptoed out of the house, through the garage, and down the drive-way to the highway to wait for Kay to pick her up. When they returned, Kay was able to pull into the driveway to drop Diana off. All she had to do was sneak into the garage and tiptoe through the kitchen to her room. She had thought about leaving the outside light on so she could see when she got back, but decided it was too risky, and stuck a small flashlight into her purse instead. Her exit and re-entry seemed rather tame compared to Lynn's.

Kay's family lived in an older home in the country that had been added onto several times. Her room had once been a mother-in-law apartment with its own bathroom and a separate entrance on the opposite side of the house from where her mom, stepdad and younger siblings slept. She used that entrance and always parked her car outside that door. The tough part for her was hoping nobody noticed that her car was missing. And nobody did.

• • •

The three of them had also skipped school several times. Diana stayed home from school whenever she felt like she needed a break, usually just to read a good book and have some quiet time, so she was an old pro at skipping school. But keeping a low profile by staying at home was way too tame for Lynn and Kay.

"Good thing they live out of town a couple of miles so nobody will notice us." Lynn commented, as Kay turned off the highway and down the driveway. She parked in front of a ranch style log house nestled amongst a grove of evergreen trees. "Do you think Diana is depressed? This is the second day this week that she's missed school."

"I don't know. But that's one of the reasons we are here, isn't it? To make sure she doesn't spend the day alone." Kay replied, matter-of-factly. Once out of the car she opened the trunk so they could stow their school books, and each of them grabbed a small duffel bag. Together they walked up to the front door and knocked.

Diana had just settled into an easy chair, propped her feet on an ottoman and opened a new library book when the knock sounded on the door. She cast a glance out the picture window to confirm her suspicions as she got to her feet, and then went to open the door. She had not been expecting Lynn and Kay to show up, but she wasn't all that surprised to see them either.

"Shame on you two for skipping school!" she scolded halfheartedly, a smile playing around her mouth. "Come on in."

"Yeah, yeah, said the pot to the kettle!" Kay agreed waving her hand in the air as if to erase Diana's comment as she and Lynn came through the door. "You know you are glad to see us. Now, we have a plan, so you need to get dressed."

"I am dressed!" Diana protested indignantly.

"Sweats are not suitable attire for a road trip!" Kay said bossily. "Get moving! We are going to change too, and then we're heading to the mall in Great Falls, so grab your cash!"

"I'm glad we just got paid, aren't you Diana?" Lynn laughed as she dug into her duffle for a change of clothes. Kay got an allowance, but Lynn and Diana both worked part-time for their spending money. "It was a stroke of genius to keep emergency outfits in your trunk, Kay!" Lynn stripped off her school clothes as she spoke.

"I was never a Girl Scout, but I do like to be prepared." Kay intoned in mock seriousness as she too, removed her school clothes.

"Maybe you should become a general since you already have a knack for giving orders." Diana called sarcastically from her bedroom. By the time Diana reappeared, dressed in jeans and a sweater with her purse slung over her shoulder, Lynn and Kay had changed into jeans and sweaters too, and had their school clothes neatly folded and stowed in their duffle bags.

"You didn't take much convincing, so you must be up for a little excitement." Kay said with a smirk.

"I've just learned from experience that it doesn't pay to argue with you when you are on a mission." Diana replied, rolling her eyes. "So I took the easy way out."

"More like you knew you were out-voted, two to one!" Lynn said as she picked up her bag.

"Yeah, that too!" Diana replied. "Which is not news; I'm always out-voted two to one. Remind me again why I continue to hang out with the two of you?"

"Either you are trying to reform us, or you need a little excitement in your life." Lynn teased.

"Whatever it takes works for me." Kay said, with a grin, as she gathered her things. "Let's go."

"So, do I even want to know how you got out this time?" Diana asked, as she closed and locked the door, and dropped the house key into her purse. "Last time one of you had an eye appointment and the other one had a migraine."

"We were absolutely brilliant, as usual!" Lynn bragged as they walked down the cobblestone path to the driveway and stowed their duffel bags in the trunk before getting into Kay's car, Diana sliding into the middle of the back seat while Lynn sat up front with Kay.

"Kay called the school office pretending to be her mother and told Mrs. Gibson that she was at home with two sick toddlers, so Kay had permission to drive herself to her orthodontic appointment. She apologized about forgetting to send a written excuse – said she'd been up most of the night and was a little out of it."

"Smart to take advantage of everyone being sick with the flu. That's going to be my excuse for tomorrow. And needless to say, the orthodontist is not expecting you." Diana commented and then turned to Lynn. "What story did you tell them?"

"It was the strangest thing! I came down with the flu right after I got to school! I guess it made me sick to see that you weren't there!" Lynn grinned over her shoulder and crossed her eyes at Diana.

"You do look a little pale." Diana teased, with a reluctant chuckle.

"Yeah, I'll have to put my makeup on again!" Lynn laughed. She turned back towards the front, extracted her makeup bag from her purse and tipped the visor down. "Try to keep the ride smooth, Kay!"

It was amazing to Diana that Lynn, and Kay too, could put make-up on in the car using the mirror on the back of the visor. Diana was so bad at applying make-up that she usually went with just mascara and lip gloss. She could manage to do that much without looking like either a clown or a hooker. She was bad at a lot of other girly things too, like applying fingernail polish and doing her hair. She always shrugged and said she needed to keep her nails short to play the piano anyway, which was true. Short nails could certainly be polished, but everyone seemed to buy her excuse so she never had to explain any further. Several times, she had been tempted to get her hair cut but long hair was easy to scrunch into a pony tail so she stuck with that. As for make-up, she read her share of make-up tips in teen magazines and had experimented in front of the mirror in her own room, but she always ended up getting frustrated and wiping everything off. She saw herself as one of those girls who were just destined to be tom-boys. She pulled her attention back to the conversation.

"Our timing and our acting were both impeccable." Kay bragged as she turned the key in the ignition. "And of course, our planning was, as always, superb!"

"What number is this in your long list of plans to get out of school?" Diana asked, curiously.

"I think we might be at an even dozen as far as the number of scenarios we've come up with. The trick is not to get too creative. We keep our excuses ordinary and nobody questions what we are doing; pretty smart of us, if I do say so myself." Kay chuckled as she turned onto the highway and increased her speed.

"Let's hear the rest of the details, then." Diana said.

"Naturally I was quite convincing as I explained that I had just thrown up in the bathroom, and I did really go in there and make retching noises before I washed off my make-up, just in case anyone noticed me. I asked Mrs. Gibson if one of my brothers could take me home because the younger kids have the flu at my house – and then I just happened to remember that both of my brothers had tests first thing this morning – luckily all of that is true. The younger kids have the flu and my brothers have tests, just in case they check." Lynn replied, gesturing with her eye-shadow brush.

"They won't, but better safe than sorry!" Kay interjected. Lynn started applying eye–shadow to her other eye as she continued her recitation.

"With her usual perfect timing, Kay came into the office at that exact moment. She looked very surprised to see me and was properly sympathetic when I told her I had the flu. After making sure they'd gotten the call from her mother so she was free to go - and of course she already knew they had, because she had made that call from the pay phone by the gym entrance - she kindly offered to give me a ride home on her way. Ain't she sweet?" Lynn finished her recitation at the same time she finished applying her eye-shadow and reached for her mascara.

"And poor Mrs. Gibson is so stressed out with all the absences that she jumped at the chance to get us off her list of things to do. It was very cool." Kay added.

"With acting talent like that, Hollywood may come calling anytime now!" Diana rolled her eyes. "One of these days, they are going to get wise to you two. Haven't they noticed that you are often gone on the same day? Funny they don't just make a phone call and check to see if the orthodontist was expecting you."

"They don't have time, and they really don't care. Anyway, you have no room to talk; this is the second time you've skipped school just this week!" Kay protested. Diana shrugged. She'd had two tests this week and that always made her tired. She never skipped on a test day, but she often stayed home on the day afterwards. She readily admitted that she missed a lot of school, but so far she wasn't flunking out, so she didn't think it mattered very much.

"I don't come up with elaborate plans though." She said quietly. "When I need a break, I just stay home for the day and read a good book or take a nap, then write an excuse that I was sick and sign my dad's name to it. No muss, no fuss – and no acting skills required."

"Which is better in what way?" Kay asked with raised eyebrows, meeting Diana's eyes briefly in the rear-view mirror. "You are still skipping school." She returned her eyes to the highway.

"Well, yeah" Diana said loftily, "But it does take away the possibility of being busted at the mall."

"Get serious!" Kay scoffed, "Great Falls is a college town. We'll blend right in with the college students."

"I hope so!" Diana muttered.

"Relax, Diana!" Lynn said as she stowed her makeup in her purse and tipped the mirror back up. She turned sideways in her seat. "You worry too much. Kay is right, nobody will notice us. Now what I was wondering, is how come your sisters haven't told your dad? They obviously know you are skipping school whenever you don't get on the bus. I can't imagine them letting you get away with that."

"Oh, they tried," Diana said with a smug look, "But I told Dad that I had cramps and he said 'oh' and let it go. Since I didn't get in trouble like they had hoped, my sisters gave up tattling on me. End of story."

"Brilliant!" Kay exclaimed. "No dad wants to discuss cramps with his teen-aged daughter! Course you can only use that excuse about once a month."

"I'm careful about that, but I also have the migraine excuse, and that one is good any time, so I'm prepared. Plus, unless my sisters say something to Dad, I don't really need an excuse for him. He leaves for work before the bus comes." Diana explained. "I just need an excuse for school, and Mrs. Gibson will believe anything you write on the excuse as long as it has what she thinks is your parent's signature."

The three friends shopped in the mall, went out for lunch, and returned to Conrad just before school was out so Lynn was not late for her after school job, and Diana was home before her sisters got off the school bus.

• • •

The only reason Diana was driving was because they were in her dad's jeep. If he knew she had taken it off-road, he probably would not be happy. She was pretty sure he sometimes drove it off-road when he went hunting, but what he did and what he would want her doing, were two different things.

At that exact moment, Diana was not particularly happy either. The three friends were in the process of fulfilling yet another activity on Kay's list of things to do before she got married. She had wondered why guys found driving off-road to be so much fun, and she wanted to try it. To go off-road, they needed a four-wheel drive vehicle, so Diana was elected to borrow her dad's jeep for the afternoon. As it happened, he was changing the oil in the station wagon, and besides, he wanted her to have more experience with a stick shift, so he didn't mind her taking the jeep to go to Kay's house.

Laughing and chatting as they bounced across the prairie with the windows down did turn out to be an enjoyable way to spend a warm sunny day. Kay had gestured vaguely in this direction when they turned off the road, and indeed there were faint tire tracks in several places. With no clear idea of where they were going, Diana had been focused on steering around rocks and shrubs, while keeping part of her mind on the conversation. When she looked up to get her bearings, she had no idea where they were. All she could see were the hills on every side of them, and the sky. The prairie was deceptive that way: it looked flat, but it was full of hills and valleys, and they seemed to be in one of those valleys. She brought the jeep to a stop.

"Where are we?" Diana muttered. Lynn and Kay stopped chatting, looked around and shrugged. Neither of them had a clue either.

"We need to go back up the hill so we can see." Kay said, even as Diana had come to the same conclusion and started turning the jeep around to retrace their path. Unfortunately, their path was too steep, so even in four wheel drive; the jeep couldn't make the grade, and it didn't help when Lynn and Kay hopped out to lighten the load. None of them realized that in order for the four wheel drive to engage, the hubs had to be locked in manually.

In silence, they contemplated their situation, and finally, Lynn suggested that they try to drive back up the hill in reverse. Diana was skeptical, but Lynn had brothers who knew an awful lot about cars, and they had nothing to lose by trying, so she moved the gearshift to reverse and eased her foot down on the gas pedal. Slowly but surely, the jeep began to chug backwards up the hill.

"Well, that was fun." Diana commented sarcastically, when they finally reached the top. She put the brake on and rolled her shoulders. "I think I have a permanent kink in my neck from looking over my shoulder."

"It's all part of the adventure, silly!" Kay retorted with a grin. "We just need to be careful not to go down any more steep hills."

"Think of it as good practice in backing up." Lynn suggested. She was grinning too. Diana said nothing, pre-occupied with wondering where they were and how to get back to the road. She searched for a landmark, but everything looked the same and with the sun high overhead, she had no sense of direction.

"Which way?" She asked as casually as she could manage, and she followed Kay's confident directions turning left at the big white rock, right at a shrub that was taller than the others, and left again at the cluster of stunted trees. She was glad the other two had kept track of the landmarks and were able to navigate by watching for them. But at the same time, she wondered why she was so unobservant that she did not notice a single one of those things until they were pointed out to her.

• • •

"You aren't going to wear that, are you?" Diana looked down at herself. Her mini-skirt had small yellow and white flowers strewn across a navy blue background, and she wore it with a scoop neck top, also in navy blue.

"What's wrong with it?"

"It doesn't match." Her sister replied with a look that said this should have been obvious. It looked fine to Diana, but her younger sister's opinion made her uncomfortable enough to return to her room and choose a different top. White went with anything, right? She tossed the navy top on the bed, and it wasn't until that evening when she picked it up to put it back in her closet that she noticed -- it was black.

• • •

Diana was scared. Her dad's station wagon was stuck in a snow drift, and it was getting dark. Her jacket wasn't heavy enough to keep her warm in sub-zero temperatures, and she had neither boots nor gloves in the car with her. In the few minutes she'd spent walking around the car to see how badly she was stuck, her toes were numb and she had started to shiver. She knew she couldn't risk leaving the car to walk for help, even if she had a clue which direction she should go. She could not see lights anywhere that would indicate there were farmhouses nearby, she had not seen any other cars on this road, and nobody knew where she was.

She'd been driving to Kay's house to work on a class project, and had decided at the last minute to take this shortcut because going through town would be a forty-five minute drive each way. It had taken half that amount of time to get from her house to Kay's house on this gravel road the previous fall, but now it was covered with snow, including a pretty good-sized snow drift that she had not seen. As she got back into the car, she wondered why it had never occurred to her that the road might be drifted in. It should have because the wind had been blowing and there were snow drifts all over the place – even in their driveway.

Well, she sighed, it wouldn't do any good to berate herself for the list of stupid things she'd done that caused her to end up here. She needed to focus on figuring out a way to get the car unstuck before she froze to death. Maybe that was a little bit dramatic. Her dad was safety conscious so the car had a full tank of gas and there was a sleeping bag in the back. She didn't think she would really freeze to death, but if she didn't get herself out of this predicament, she would definitely spend a very uncomfortable night and she didn't want her dad to worry.

She remembered watching him rock the car back and forth last year when he was stuck in the driveway, so she decided to try that. After some trial and error, she figured out how to shift between forward and reverse to gently rock the car forward and backward without spinning the tires. Very slowly, she worked her way backwards out of the snow drift. Holding tightly to the steering wheel as she peered through the windshield looking for more snowdrifts, she proceeded cautiously to Kay's house. She returned home through town, and in fact, never used that particular short cut again.

Diana did not mention this incident to either of her friends, and wouldn't have told her dad either, except that there was no other way to explain how the muffler had gotten torn off. He gave her a stern look and said he guessed she'd just learned firsthand why it was important to keep the gas tank full, especially in the winter. That was all he said, and then he replaced the muffler. From that day, Diana always made sure someone knew where she was headed and what route she planned to take, and she made sure she dressed for the weather, just in case.

CHAPTER 3

Clues

• • •

"DIANA?" HER DATE SHOOK HER shoulder gently. Diana opened her eyes and realized that she had fallen asleep on the ride home from the dance. Again. The strobe light had given her a headache. How people could see with those flashes of light pulsing in time to the music she didn't know, but they blinded her and made her head hurt. The headache was directly attributable to the strobe light, but falling asleep on the drive home from a date was normal for her. It didn't matter who she went out with or what they did, she couldn't seem to stay awake on the drive home. So far she hadn't drooled on herself, and she sincerely hoped that she didn't snore.

One guy had asked if she fell asleep because he was so boring. She assured him that he wasn't, and though she didn't say it out loud, she wouldn't have continued to spend time with someone who was boring. That thought led her to wonder why he had asked her out a second time. Maybe she was the one who was boring when she fell asleep on a date.

Sometimes she was just so tired she couldn't keep her eyes open. It was the same kind of overwhelming exhaustion that pulled at her if she had a week with a big test or a research paper to do. Her friends had noticed how often she skipped school and some of them thought she was depressed. She scoffed at the idea, but she also read a couple of articles about depression, and the information in them plus their worries made her uneasy enough to go see the doctor. Not that she mentioned depression, of course. She told the doctor that she was tired a lot, which was true enough, and he ran a couple of tests. She wasn't anemic and didn't have an infection, so her doctor visit ruled out a couple of things, without solving the problem. Her friends were still worried, and she didn't know why she was so tired. She didn't feel depressed.

She also read articles about the research being done on stress and thought maybe she didn't handle things as well as everyone else did. To begin with, she thought it was normal that tests and research papers gave her headaches and left her exhausted but then she realized that school work didn't have that effect on her friends. She figured maybe it was eye strain, but the optometrist said her glasses didn't need to be changed. So she wondered if perhaps she was just not as smart as everyone else and had to work harder. That idea was a little depressing since she had always considered herself to be fairly bright, but how would she know, really? Maybe she had to work harder at her studies, and the overwhelming fatigue showed up when she relaxed and had fun, and that was why she fell asleep on dates. With a mental shrug, she added it to her growing list of things that she didn't understand.

• • •

Diana and Lynn, both sophomores at MSU in Bozeman, were on their way home to Conrad for Thanksgiving. It seemed like whenever they headed home for a weekend or a holiday, someone always needed a ride, so there were two girls from one of Lynn's classes in the back seat. They hadn't left Bozeman until six, and all of them were tired from finals so they were taking turns driving. Diana got behind the wheel in Helena. When they came to Wolf Creek Canyon, they encountered a detour marked with sand filled fluorescent orange and white striped barrels. Diana felt her shoulders tense as she slowed her speed and maneuvered carefully around the barrels. She had just breathed a sigh of relief at the end of the gravel detour, when suddenly another barrel materialized on her right and she jerked the wheel to the left in an attempt to avoid hitting it. Thwack!

"Oh!" Lynn exclaimed from the other side of the front seat. "I think we hit something!" Diana had already stopped the car, and she and the two girls in the backseat piled out to see what the damage was. Lynn had to slide under the steering wheel because the door on her side wouldn't open. The only damage appeared to be the barrel-shaped dent that now marred the appearance of the passenger door; no wonder it wouldn't open! There was nothing to be done about it, so the girls piled back into the car and continued on their way, with Lynn behind the wheel because Diana was so upset.

"I'm so sorry!" Diana said, for at least the seventh time. "I thought we were through the construction zone! I can't believe I didn't see that last barrel! I hope it doesn't cost too much to get the door fixed."

"Oh, don't worry; my brothers can get the dent out of the door." Lynn assured her. "We were all laughing and singing with the radio, so we probably distracted you. Good thing you weren't going very fast."

"Yeah," Diana muttered. "But I can't believe I didn't see that barrel. It glows in the dark, for Pete's sake!"

"Relax, nobody was hurt." Lynn soothed and there were murmurs of agreement from the back seat. But Diana was not soothed. She was positive that she had been paying close attention and that she had not been distracted by the other girls. She had been as focused and alert as she knew how to be, and it had not prevented her second accident in three years. She stared moodily out at the darkness beyond the passenger window and wondered if she was just a terrible driver.

She continued to drive, of course, because driving was part of life as she knew it, but she was very, very careful. After several years without any more accidents, she decided that her caution and practice had improved her driving skill and the worry that she was a terrible driver was pushed to the back of her mind, mostly gone but not entirely forgotten.

• • •

Diana took inventory of her body parts, decided she wasn't seriously hurt, and got gingerly to her feet. There was no blood, but her right shoulder and hip were going to be sore. That was still better than a head injury, and she supposed she should be grateful for her love of gymnastics. Thanks to her time on the mats, she had instinctively tucked and rolled.

Everything had happened so fast! One minute she was pedaling up the hill on her ten-speed, and the next she was sprawled on the edge of the street. Her bike lay on its side but it didn't appear to be damaged. She picked it up and waited for her hands to stop shaking while she studied the area where she had wrecked. She couldn't see anything that should have caused her to crash. No obstacles, no pothole – nothing – and yet there had to be some reason! She looked closer and saw a barely discernible ridge where the cement curb and gutter met the asphalt street. Surely that tiny ridge couldn't have caused her to go flying over the handlebars of her bike?

She sighed and shook her head as she swung a leg over the bar and put her foot on the pedal, wondering if she should re-think her latest idea for saving money while she worked her way through college. Her previous summer jobs had included babysitting, cleaning, and working in a store, but this year she was working outdoors for the city park system. So far she had raked, mowed, planted flowers, done some weeding, and sanded picnic tables to be repainted. She didn't have to dress up and would get dirty and sweaty anyway, so she thought biking to and from work would be good exercise and save gas money. If she wasn't more careful, it would be a good way to break her neck!

• • •

Grayson Tucker unlocked the door to room 122 at the Holiday Inn. He and Diana had come to Bozeman so he could attend a continuing education seminar. After a grueling two days of classes, it had been great to unwind over dinner and a few beers with friends. Diana walked past him and picked up two envelopes from the desk.

"I'll be right back," she said, "I want to mail these."

"Now?" he asked, looking at his watch and then at her with raised eyebrows.

"I don't want to forget." She said with a smile. She slipped off the sandals that had been pinching her little toe for the past three hours and then turned towards the door.

Gray and Diana met at wedding just before their senior year in college and were married shortly after graduation. He supposed they could still be considered newlyweds, since they had been married just over six months. Gray thought he was adjusting to some of the odd things Diana did, so he refrained from asking why she had taken her sandals off if she planned to walk down to the lobby. He had no idea why she needed to mail those cards now instead of in the morning, because he was pretty sure the mail in the lobby wasn't going to be picked up tonight. This was a weekend, after all. He shrugged and turned on the television.

Diana walked barefoot down the hall following the signs directing her towards the lobby. Rounding the corner, she paused to get her bearings. She hadn't realized that the lobby was on the other side of the pool area, and even though it was nearly midnight, there seemed to be a party going on.

Well, she thought, spring was graduation time. She briefly considered whether to turn back or continue on, and decided to follow through with her plan. All of the party goers seemed to be occupied and in any case they were on the far side of the pool area. She tried to be unobtrusive as she moved forward. Thinking it would be very embarrassing to fall into the pool, she gave it a wide berth, and breathed a small sigh of relief when she got past it. She was nearly to the lobby and she didn't think she'd even been noticed by the raucous party crowd.

She guesstimated that there were about thirty of them, and all of them were men. Maybe it was a bachelor party, she mused. And the next thing she knew, she was struggling for balance in the middle of the wading pool. All the talking and laughter on the other side of the room ceased immediately, so she was pretty sure everyone heard her exclamation.

"Shit!"

She had stumbled forward to keep her balance. While she was certainly grateful that she hadn't fallen on her face, she knew that her face was now beet-red with embarrassment. Not a sound came from the group of men who stood in a frozen tableau, their eyes glued to her. As nonchalantly as possible, she waded to the edge of the wading pool and stepped out. She was grateful that the wading pool wasn't deep so she was spared the indignity of having to crawl out, but her long, pale blue princess style dress was soaked from the knees down. If there was a silver lining in this cloud, it was that she'd taken off her brand new white leather sandals.

She kept her chin up as she walked barefooted into the lobby and slipped the cards through the mail slot. The desk clerk gave her a preoccupied smile and went back to his book. He was probably a college student studying for finals. Thankfully, his view of her was blocked by the front desk, and she was relieved to see that the lobby was deserted. She glanced towards the main doors, thinking she could go outside, around the building and re-enter through the door from the parking area. She realized at once that she did not have a room key, and all the doors except the one for the main lobby would be locked. Not to mention that she wasn't wearing shoes.

With no choice but to walk back the way she had come, she sighed and squaring her shoulders, took a deep breath and faked a bravado she certainly did not feel. The standing ovation, complete with wolf-whistles, hooting, applause, and foot stomping began when she took her first step into the pool area and continued until she reached the hall on the other side. Even with her face flaming, she couldn't resist a jaunty little wave over her shoulder just before she turned the corner into the hallway. Might as well play the part, she thought ruefully.

Gray answered her knock on the door, took one look at her dress, which had stopped dripping, but was still wet, and raised his eyebrows.

"I managed not to fall into the pool." Diana said with a shrug, "But I didn't see the wading pool." Gray tried unsuccessfully to smother a snicker.

"How could you not see the wading pool if you saw the swimming pool?" he asked.

"Good question." Diana replied. Then she told him about the guys who had cheered her return trip through the pool area, and he laughed til tears ran down his face. The next morning, Gray suggested they go somewhere else for breakfast. Diana protested that the hotel had a nice restaurant.

"Yeah, but here you might be recognized." He reminded her.

● ● ●

"What happened to your hand?" Gray asked, noticing that her left hand was red and glistened with some kind of ointment. She shrugged.

"I spilled coffee on it."

"How did you manage that?"

"I just wasn't paying attention, I guess. I had the thermos in my left hand and the coffeepot in my right hand, and some coffee splashed on my hand." Diana shrugged.

"How bad is it?"

"Not bad. I soaked it in cold water and then put some aloe vera on it." She wrote the incident off as not paying attention, but ever afterwards, she put the thermos in the sink and filled it without having her left hand anywhere near the stream of hot coffee from the coffee pot.

● ● ●

Diana loved movies, but Gray wasn't much of a movie goer. Somehow, the kids had talked him into going to see "Star Wars" and "The Empire Strikes Back" and he had enjoyed them both. So when "Return of the Jedi" hit their local theater they decided to go see it as a family.

As expected, the boys went off to sit with their friends as soon as Gray bought their tickets and paid for their popcorn. Just as Diana stepped into the theatre, the lights went out, and the previews of coming attractions flashed up on the screen. Disoriented by the sudden darkness coupled with the glare from the screen, she reached out to touch the seat on her right in order to get her bearings. Instead of the seat back, she touched someone's shoulder, and there was a gasp as the man occupying that seat apparently thought she was getting a little too friendly. She whispered an apology at the same time Gray took her arm and pulled her down the aisle. Diana laughed it off and insisted it was an innocent mistake on her part.

● ● ●

"For heaven's sake! Nobody is going to check the dye-lot on your socks!" Diana said sarcastically, as she watched Gray re-sort the socks she had just put into his drawer. He frequently complained that she mismatched his socks. He didn't think she did it on purpose; he thought she might be colorblind. She thought he was being a jerk.

One afternoon, their first grade son Riley was telling her about his day at school while she finished folding a basket of clean clothes. He was in the middle of a sentence, when he stopped and pointed to a pair of socks she had just matched up.

"Those aren't the same." He said. She frowned.

"They're not?"

"No." He shook his head, clearly wondering if she was teasing him.

"But they're both black."

"Yeah, but this one is blacker than that one." Riley explained, pointing. She let him finish sorting the socks. In fact, she told Gray that she had decided to resign from sock-sorting completely. She didn't take any classes in it at college, it wasn't in the fine print on the marriage contract, and it wasn't included in her job description!

It was not the first time, nor would it be the last that Diana used humor to mask what she saw as her many and varied inadequacies. She knew she wasn't color blind, exactly, but she also knew that sometimes she couldn't distinguish between navy and black, and apparently, between shades of black.

• • •

Diana rolled over in bed and squinted at the clock, or at least she thought she was looking towards the spot where the clock radio rested on the bedside table on her husband's side of the bed. Why she bothered, she didn't know, because usually she couldn't see it. The whole idea behind the inch high red digital numerals that glowed in the dark was to be able to see what time it was in the middle of the night. But for some reason, it didn't seem to work for her. She let her eyes scan the entire side of the room, and there it was – a flash of red. She looked towards it, and saw nothing but blackness. She scanned the area again and saw another flash of red. Again she was unable to find it when she looked straight at where she thought it should be. Irritated now, she scanned that area of the room three more times, each time catching a glimpse of red, and finally she was able to pinpoint the location of the digital numbers. It was four twelve a.m. and she was wide-awake, which is what usually happened when she had a mini-temper tantrum in the middle of the night. She had gotten upset several times when she couldn't see what time it was, and it was beyond dumb to have just done it again. Seriously, what difference did it make if she could tell what time it was in the middle of the night? Obviously, it wasn't time to get up because it was still pitch dark outside. Sometimes the things that she couldn't do made her mad, and then she was determined to do them just to prove that she could. Her stubbornness had just cost her a couple of hours of sleep!

• • •

"Diana?" Gray called as he came out of the bedroom with a pair of socks in his hands.

"Hm?" Diana answered distractedly as she perused the comics in the morning paper.

"What is this?" He held out his socks for her to see. She glanced at the socks and then went back to the comics.

"Those are socks, dear."

"Very funny!" Gray rolled his eyes. "What are these colored threads for?"

"Oh. I marked them." Diana replied.

"Why?" Gray asked.

"Because I can't tell the difference between the black ones and the navy ones!" She was beginning to get annoyed.

"You can't?"

"No." She said shortly, and put the paper down.

"What good does the red thread do?"

"The navy socks have red thread. The black ones have white thread. That way I can match them up according to the color of thread in the toes."

"What about the other colors?" Gray asked.

" I don't have trouble with brown, gray or tan." At least not yet, she added to herself.

"How could you tell which color was which so you could mark them?" He persisted, and she blew out a frustrated breath.

"I only did it on the new ones I bought last week – and I did it before I took the labels off." She admitted with a sigh. He gave her a funny look and returned to the bedroom to finish getting dressed for work. When she came up with the idea, she had thought it was a brilliant way to sort socks. She should have known that he would notice and ask her about it. Gray didn't miss much.

• • •

Diana was on her way home from a church meeting in Valier. She always drove too fast, and this day was no exception. Montana's speed limit was "reasonable and prudent" and Diana thought that on a clear fall day, when the pavement was dry and there was very little traffic, it was perfectly reasonable to be whizzing down the interstate at eighty-five miles per hour. Prudent wasn't something she was going to think about. She was about three miles from the Shelby exit off the interstate when the car sputtered and died. Without thinking about it she slipped the automatic gearshift into neutral and glanced down at her gauges. She distinctly remembered checking the gas gauge before she left home that morning, and could have sworn she had half a tank. That would have been more than enough to get her the forty miles or so to Valier and back. Obviously, she had misread the gauge because now it showed that the tank was empty. She figured that the closer she got to town before the car actually stopped -- the shorter the distance she would have to walk. As the car continued to coast, she pulled over onto the shoulder so she wouldn't obstruct traffic. Not that there was any traffic. Wouldn't you know that when she might need a ride, there wasn't a car in sight in either direction!

There was a small incline before the interstate headed downhill towards the Shelby exit. When she reached it the car was barely moving and Diana had the steering wheel in a death grip and was leaning forward muttering, "Come on! Come on!" as if her words could urge the car forward. But maybe it helped, because the car inched over the crest of the hill and then slowly began to pick up speed as it rolled down the off ramp to where it joined Highway 2 at the edge of town. Diana was able to merge right, coast to the truck stop, and pull up beside the gas pump.

It took several moments to unclamp her fingers from the steering wheel so she could retrieve her gas card from her purse, get out of the car, and fill the tank. When she pumped the gas pedal a couple of times and turned the key, the engine fired, coughed a couple of times, and settled into its customary purr.

Later when she recounted her adventure to Gray, he shook his head and said her guardian angels must work overtime. Diana thought those guardian angels could save themselves – and her -- a lot of grief if they could just find a way to help her read the gas gauge correctly.

● ● ●

Diana stood staring at the mess she'd just made in the kitchen. She had intended to place her cold drink on the table, but instead her glass had plummeted to the floor where it smashed into at least a thousand pieces. Shaking her head in disgust, she reached for the roll of paper towels to sop up the puddle of iced tea and the shards of broken glass.

"Wouldn't you think," she muttered, speaking to herself since she was the only one in the room, "That I would remember to make sure the glass was actually on the table before letting go of it?" Nobody answered.

After sopping up the worst of the mess, she got out the broom and dust pan, and then she used the vacuum. Finally, she used the mop; fairly certain the floor was no longer sticky, but worried that she might have missed a piece of glass.

CHAPTER 4

More Clues

• • •

"WHAT ARE YOU LOOKING FOR?" Kay asked. They were at Lynn's home and she had found Diana staring at the floor in the kitchen.

"I dropped an earring." Diana replied. Kay looked at the floor.

"There it is." Kay said, pointing. Diana didn't move. "Don't you see it?"

"Uh, no." Diana muttered.

"It's by your left foot." Diana shook her head in frustration. Kay bent down, retrieved the earring and handed it to her.

"Maybe you need your glasses changed, huh?" Kay joked.

"Yeah, maybe." Diana replied. But she'd had an eye exam last month and the prescription for her lenses hadn't changed. She had been looking at the floor right by her feet, so she must have been looking right at the dropped earring, without seeing it. How was that possible?

• • •

"We made it." Diana said into the telephone at her grandmother's house in Eastern Montana. She was exhausted. Driving for nearly eight hours with three kids wasn't her idea of a good time, but her grandparents weren't getting any younger and her children were growing up fast, so she tried to make this trip once a year. She had gotten a late start on this particular day. Stopping for lunch gave them all a break from being in the car, but it also took nearly an hour, and combined with the late start, and the rain, they didn't arrive in Culbertson until after dark.

"I was starting to get worried." Gray replied. "I thought you'd be there quite awhile ago."

"Me too. The only thing worse than me driving in the dark, is me driving in the dark when it's raining." Diana replied soberly. "It took a little longer."

"You'll drive home in the daylight?"

"Count on it!"

• • •

"There's Amtrak" Gray said. They always made a game of watching for the passenger train whenever they drove between West Glacier and East Glacier in the evening. Amtrak was supposed to leave Shelby in the late afternoon, but it wasn't always on time, so sometimes they saw it and sometimes they didn't. Besides not knowing if it was on time, the train tracks winding through the mountains were not always visible from the highway.

"How do you know it isn't a freighter?" Diana asked, as her eyes searched the dusky semi-darkness on both sides of the highway. She didn't know which side of the road the tracks were on because she wasn't sure where they were.

"Because of the lights." Gray said, just as Diana caught a glimpse of the lighted windows of the passenger train off to the left and above the road.

"I guess you win this time." She commented blandly. Who was she kidding? He always spotted Amtrak first. In fact, sometimes she didn't see the passenger train at all, even after he told her which side of the road it was on. But then, she didn't see a lot of the things he pointed out on their drives; last week she had missed the bald eagle in the tree top and she rarely saw deer or elk unless they crossed the highway in front of them. Well, she consoled herself, she still enjoyed sunsets, and she could eventually find the moon when it rose in the night sky.

• • •

Diana walked out of the store beside the box boy who was pushing the cart containing her groceries and looked around for the pickup. She didn't see it, which was odd because there were only about a dozen vehicles in the parking lot just then. As the box boy gave her a questioning look, no doubt wondering which car was hers, she scanned the lot again, wondering if she was losing her memory.

Masking her confusion by fumbling for the keys, she accidentally hit the alarm button. The noise was deafening, but something good came of it because Diana realized that she had been looking for their black pickup, but it was her car that sat in the middle of the parking lot with blinking lights and honking horn. As she de-activated the alarm she decided to wait until later to worry about how her gaze had managed to pass right over her bright red car – not just once, but several times - without recognizing it. She led the way towards the now silent car as casually as if this happened all the time. Odd things did happen to her on a regular basis, though this particular thing had not happened before.

"Those alarms are so handy when you can't remember where you parked." She said with a perfectly straight face, completely ignoring the box boy's startled look. It didn't matter to her if he thought she was a crazy lady. Most days, including this one, she was convinced that she was a millimeter away from completely losing it. Did other people spend fifteen minutes in the grocery store and forget what vehicle they were driving? Did they look right past the vehicle they have been driving for a couple of years - several times - without realizing it was theirs? She didn't know, and quite frankly, she was afraid to pursue the answer to the question. She could only hope the box boy wouldn't tell this story to his friends. Because Shelby was a small town, so if he told people, her kids would undoubtedly hear about it.

• • •

When she and Gray were growing up, neither of their families could afford to snow ski. That was one of the reasons they wanted their children to learn. After a couple of lessons, the kids were zipping down the slope like pros, while Diana was still struggling not to have a heart attack every time she got on or off the lift. She didn't know if Gray skied with her because he was at a similar level of expertise, or if he was just worried about her killing herself or someone else.

Diana didn't think sliding downhill on her back, head first, struggling to her feet and then looking for her skis, could actually be defined as skiing. It was more than a little frustrating because she had always been pretty coordinated and she enjoyed sports. That was why she'd gotten a minor in physical education at MSU.

Even though skiing was difficult and frustrating, it was still wonderful to be outdoors spending time with her family. That is, if riding to the ski hill in the same car, paying the equipment rental fees, and riding home in the same vehicle, could be construed as family time. She asked Gray for his opinion as they waited in the lift line. He laughed.

"Don't forget that the kids tracked us down so we could buy them lunch, and we'll probably stop for pizza on the way home, so that's two meals together."

Towards the end of the day, Diana and Gray had decided to take one more run. She was excited because she had finally managed the last two runs without falling. Within a few minutes, she would think that she should have quit while she was ahead.

She somehow managed to get her skis crossed as they stood waiting for the lift, so when she tried to move forward, she fell over. Gray helped her untangle her skis and get back up with a minimum of eye-rolling.

She was still flustered when it was their turn to get on the chair, and she convinced herself that was the reason she fell again and they had to stop the lift and help her get sorted out. Gray did not talk to her on the way up the hill, so she figured he was a little irritated. When she fell getting off the lift too, and he did not offer to help her up, there was no doubt in her mind that he had reached the upper level of his tolerance. Apparently he regained his sense of humor because he gave the boys all the gory details over dinner, and they laughed until they nearly choked on their pizza.

• • •

Gray was out of town or Diana would have asked him to pick the boys up from their youth group meeting. It had rained all day and the wet streets seemed to absorb the car headlights, making it even harder for her to see. With her head pounding, she drove slowly and carefully across town, thankful that they didn't live in a city where traffic would be more of a problem. By the time she pulled to the curb in front of the youth leader's house, her stomach was threatening to revolt and she suspected she was on the edge of a migraine.

"Mark, do you think you could drive home?" She said when the boys got into the car.

"Sure," He replied confidently. He was thirteen and Gray had been letting him do a bit of practice driving on country roads. Gray might have done that anyway, but Diana had not forgotten how it felt to be one of the few with no driving experience during driver's education classes. Teaching Mark to drive had been her suggestion. Even so, he had not driven in town and did not have a license, so what she was asking him to do was illegal and maybe unsafe. Or maybe not, she thought, as she moved into the passenger seat and made sure Cole and Riley had fastened their seat belts in the back seat. Maybe she was the one who, tonight at least, would be an unsafe driver.

"Be really careful, okay?" she directed with her eyes nearly closed, head and heart both pounding. She needn't have worried. Mark had no trouble navigating the short distance back to their house and parking the car. Diana's headache did indeed morph into a migraine within a half hour or so and she rationalized that as the reason she had felt unable to drive on that particular night.

• • •

Two years later, when Mark got his driver's license, Diana encouraged him to drive at every opportunity. While other kids his age were begging to drive, she handed him the keys before he had a chance to ask and willingly occupied the passenger seat. She told him that she just wanted him to get as much experience as possible so he'd be a good driver. Well, that was part of it, but if she was being completely honest, and she did try to be completely honest, at least with herself, she did not like to drive.

• • •

Gray bought Diana a mountain bike for her fortieth birthday. Like most people her age, she grew up before training wheels were common. She was six when she learned to ride a bike with her dad holding on to the seat until she got her balance. That second-hand bike had a big seat, high handlebars, no gears, and she had to share it with her sister, but it was a wonderful way to travel around the neighborhood.

In college, she had a sleek shiny ten-speed that she rode for fun and used as transportation to and from her landscaping job one summer. It was a great way to keep her legs toned so they looked good in those mini-skirts that were so popular.

The first few times she took her birthday bike out, she was so wobbly that she wondered if the old adage about never forgetting how to ride a bike was true. She studied muscle memory in college as part of her physical education curriculum, but she didn't remember reading anything about muscle memory getting old and forgetful, though if it was anything like mental memory, she supposed it did. That's probably where the saying "use it or lose it" came from. Still, each time she went for a bike ride, she wobbled a little less, her muscles were not quite as sore afterwards, and her confidence grew.

Then one day, for no apparent reason, she wrecked. It happened on a quiet, level street with no obstructions or distractions. Her mind flashed back to similar accidents when she was in college. As she picked herself up and retrieved her bike, she glanced around and could find no reason for her fall. She eventually concluded that she must have had a moment of brain fog and gotten careless. The good news was that her muscle memory enabled her to automatically tuck and roll. Other than a few bruises, and muscles that would be sore the next day, she wasn't hurt.

She continued to ride her bike, albeit without quite as much enjoyment, throughout that summer and the next, watching carefully for potholes, rocks and twigs, or anything else that might cause her to sail over the handlebars. Eventually she stopped riding the bike, still without knowing the cause of what she privately referred to as her random wrecks. It was easier to think she was clumsy and/or careless than it was to worry about the possibility that she was having mini-strokes or suffering from some kind of neurological disorder.

• • •

Gray and Diana went to Bozeman to attend an MSU football game. They planned to drive home Saturday night after the game, stopping for dinner along the way. Riley, a high school junior, volunteered to hand out candy to trick-or-treaters on Saturday night before he went out with his friends. Just because he was a good kid, didn't mean Diana didn't worry about him. She said she would call him when they were on their way home to check on him, and asked him to keep the bag phone handy.

Bag phones were the pre-curser to personal cell phones. About the size of a three ring binder, they had a handset attached to the base by a coiled cord like a wall phone, and they plugged into the cigarette lighter in the car. They got their name because they usually zipped into a case, or bag. They were bulky but functional, and the Tucker family owned two of them.

Gray and Diana enjoyed the football game, but Diana called home several times to check on Riley, who assured her that he hadn't burned the house down or been arrested. Well, you can't blame a mother for worrying about her kids, Diana thought defensively.

When they were about half-way home on Saturday evening, Diana dialed their other bag phone from the one she and Gray had in their car and got a busy signal. She tried again a few minutes later with the same result. When, over the next hour she kept getting a busy signal, she began to fume. All of their kids had been cautioned that the bag phone was only for staying in touch with their parents or for emergencies. They were not to be used for social calls. There were two reasons for this rule, one being that the phone service was expensive, and the other being that Diana wanted to keep the line available in case it was needed for something important. At that moment, Diana was trying to get Riley on the phone and she assumed that he was using the phone to chat with his friends. This made her furious, and she vented to Gray the rest of the way home. The house phone rang just a few minutes after they walked into their house.

"Mom," Riley said, "I thought you were going to call on your way home. I was starting to get worried about you guys." Diana barely heard him.

"I've been trying to call you for two hours and all I got was a busy signal," Diana said angrily. "You aren't supposed to…" but Riley interrupted.

"Mom! Mom! Wait!"

"What??" Diana snapped.

"What number did you call?" he asked. Diana didn't answer and he repeated the question. "What number did you call?"

"Five-One-Five-Zero." She replied, still puzzled.

"That's the phone you guys had, Mom. I've got the other one."

"What?" Diana said.

"You got a busy signal because you were dialing your own number." Riley explained. Diana was so stunned that she hung up on him. How could she have gotten the two phones mixed up? They were similar in appearance, sure, but they were not identical. One was older than the other, slightly bulkier, and the black covering was noticeably faded from exposure to the sun. The two phones had been sitting side by side on the counter when she packed the car and she distinctly remembered being careful to look at both of them so she would take the more faded one. She picked up the receiver of the wall phone and dialed the prefix and then the number of the other phoneme: one-seven-three, and sure enough, Riley answered.

"I can't believe it! You were right, Riley." Diana apologized. "I'm sorry I yelled at you. It never occurred to me that I might have mixed the phones up."   And she never did figure out how she'd done that.

• • •

Diana's dad had recently been diagnosed with Parkinson's disease and dementia and had been staying with her youngest sister in California for several months. The two sisters hoped that Marcy could look after him in the winter and Diana could take care of him in the summer. That plan went out the window the first week in January when Marcy called one morning to report that his dementia had worsened to the point that he no longer recognized her, and thought her house was an airport. Diana agreed to come and get him, and made her travel arrangements as soon as she got off the phone with Marcy.

The flight to California that afternoon was uneventful, but the flight back the next day with her dad was a nightmare. Weather delays caused them to miss their connecting flight in Salt Lake City, and they were stuck in the airport for several hours waiting for the next one. Duane kept wandering off, and though he didn't resist her directions, Diana wasn't entirely sure if he knew who she was. When they finally got to Great Falls at nine thirty p.m., their luggage was lost, it was snowing, and the combination of low temperatures and wind made the chill factor a frigid fifty degrees below zero. Diana counted it a blessing when the car started. While waiting for the engine to warm up, she heard a buzzing noise and realized her dad was rolling down his window.

"What are you doing, Dad?" She asked, as she used the controls on her door to roll his window back up, shutting out the howling wind and snow flurries.

"I'm trying to help you fly this thing." He replied, adjusting his seat and then flipping the visor down and back up. Marcy had warned her that he hallucinated, or at least he misinterpreted what he saw, imagining and describing aloud some pretty outlandish things, like a two-headed calf grazing on her lawn, and brightly colored snakes where his shoelaces should have been. She had also said he didn't seem to be sleeping well and he wandered around at night. He had to be exhausted, Diana thought, because she certainly was. She rubbed her forehead and tried to think what to say to soothe him.

"This plane has auto-pilot. As soon as we get underway, it pretty much flies itself. You can rest."

"Oh. Okay." He replied and leaned back against the headrest. He was asleep before the engine finished warming up. Clutching the steering wheel tightly, Diana drove slowly and carefully out of the airport parking lot and towards the interstate onramp. She had been trying to avoid night driving for the past couple of years, and if the flight had been on time, she would have been home by the time it got dark. Instead, the flight was five hours late, and she was afraid to check into a motel for fear her dad would wake up and wander off in the middle of the night. She consoled herself that it was interstate all the way from Great Falls to Shelby, so she didn't have to worry too much about the glare from oncoming traffic.

There were plenty of other things to worry about. The wind was blowing, the gusts stirring up flurries of snow to obscure her vision. She knew the road was mostly straight and she took it slow, holding her breath whenever a car passed and stirred the snow up so visibility dropped to zero for several heart-stopping moments. The ninety mile trip took over two hours and as she pulled into Shelby, she breathed a sigh of relief to be home safe. With her next breath, she vowed to never again drive at night, and to make sure she kept that vow, she told everyone in her family.

• • •

Cole asked what made her decide her days of night driving were over.

"You know those rides at Disneyland where you are in a little car and everything is dark and then stuff flies at you from all directions?"

"Yeah."

"It's like that." Diana explained.

"What kind of stuff comes at you?" He persisted, looking worried.

"Oh, lights from other cars or the cement supports from the over-passes, or road signs." She replied.

"So when you see a road sign, it seems like it comes at you, suddenly?" He asked. "Out of nowhere?"

"Yeah. At night all I see are the lines on the road in my head-lights, and then all of a sudden there will be a sign or an overpass. It's unnerving."

"Good decision, to stop driving at night." He said, soberly.

• • •

With their last child off to college, Gray and Diana had a free weekend. They were so accustomed to attending high school sporting events that it felt a little weird to be at loose ends. They decided to drive to Great Falls, go out for dinner and see a movie. The theatre was packed, but the usher assured them that there were two seats towards the front. The previews were showing as they made their way in the direction the usher gestured. Diana could not see anything at all because of the glare from the screen, so she kept ahold of Gray's arm and when he whispered to sit down, she sat. Oops! Unfortunately, that seat was already occupied and Diana ended up on a strange man's lap. She jumped up with a heartfelt whispered apology, and the man was really nice about it, but his wife did not seem understanding at all. Diana got the distinct impression from the furious whispering she overheard, that without meaning to, she had caused a problem between the couple they sat beside during the movie. She tried to apologize again when the lights came up after the movie, but the woman made a bee-line for the exit and refused to listen.

Gray explained later that he'd been pointing at the seat next to the one the man was in. Diana just shook her head. If he knew she couldn't see the seats, how did he expect her to see where he was pointing? She doubted they'd be going to another movie anytime soon.

● ● ●

Their kids had arrived late the previous night, home from college for the Christmas holiday, and they weren't up yet. Diana was still in her bathrobe while she and Gray sat at the table in the kitchen, reading the paper and drinking coffee. She finished with the comics and decided to get dressed. When she walked right into the closed wooden door between the kitchen and the dining room, the sound reverberated through the house like a rifle shot.

"Why did you shut the door?" Diana hissed at Gray.

"The kids were still asleep; I was trying to be quiet." He replied, staring at her.

"I bet they aren't asleep now!" She said angrily.

"Probably not."

"You should have told me you closed it!" She huffed, even as she privately acknowledged that there was no reason he should have told her he was closing a door that was in plain sight of the table where she was sitting. She wondered if she'd been looking right at him when he did that. It was entirely possible.

"Are you hurt?" Gray asked.

"No." Diana sighed, rubbing her forehead.

"I still don't see how you could just run into the door like that." Gray shook his head.

"I think 'see' is the operative word here! I didn't see it, okay?" Diana snapped, and then she sighed and explained in a quieter tone, "I guess I didn't look where I was going."

"What happened?"

"What was that noise?"

"What's going on?" Their three sons were certainly not asleep anymore, and none of them understood how someone could walk into a closed door in broad daylight, either. Diana couldn't explain it, and wondering about it gave her a worse headache than the one she had from running into the door.

• • •

Diana drove to the theatre, parked the car, and went in. She had decided to attend the one--thirty showing of "Harry Potter and the Prisoner of Azkaban." After she sat on that stranger's lap, she had persuaded Gray to take her to see the first two Harry Potter movies, but he was a complete Star Wars fan and he just couldn't get interested in the wizarding world. Diana had not been a regular movie goer in many years, but she had attended countless movies by herself in her younger days, and she decided to see the next Harry Potter movie without him.

The theatre seemed a little darker than she remembered, and it was a bit of a challenge to find her seat, but she got there, settled in with her popcorn and thoroughly enjoyed the movie. She waited until the lights came up before making her way out to the lobby, and in hindsight, she probably should have waited a few more minutes before trying to walk from the dimly lit lobby into the late afternoon sunlight. Perhaps if she'd done that, she wouldn't have walked smack into the glass wall strategically placed right beside the glass door, making about the same sound birds make when they fly into a picture window. The impact knocked her glasses askew, and bruised her forehead, her nose, and her ego. It probably also made people wonder if she was under the influence of drink or drugs. But on the bright side, she didn't break her neck like those poor birds usually did.

She assured the theatre personnel that she was fine and made her way through the parking lot to her car, where she sat for several minutes until she felt like she could drive. She tried -- and failed -- to convince herself that her latest faux pas been the theatre's fault for keeping the glass so clean, or for having a glass wall to begin with. Nope. It was pretty clear that something was wrong with either her eyes or her brain.

CHAPTER 5

Epiphany

• • •

DIANA SPENT A WEEK IN the Seattle area visiting friends shortly after her fifty-fifth birthday. At Gray's suggestion she had also made an appointment at a well-known alternative medicine clinic. In spite of a relatively healthy diet, moderate exercise, and an assortment of self-prescribed supplements, Diana never seemed to have much energy and Gray was worried about her.

According to the three different physicians she had seen in the previous three years, each of whom had given her a physical, she was in good health for her age. What that meant, she wasn't sure, but she still qualified for the "good" rather than the "poor" health category on whatever scale they used for insurance physicals.

She was tired of trying new things and not interested in consulting with a doctor about her health. Since she had already lived with her low energy for most of her life, she figured she could continue to do so. She had, in fact, decided that adjusting to her limitations was preferable to becoming a whiner who ran from doctor to doctor with a list of vague complaints for which there didn't seem to be a treatment or a cure.

Gray thought it would be better to consult with a natural health practitioner who specialized in Nutrition Response Therapy (NRT). Both of them believed more in prevention than in cures, especially if those cures involved pharmaceuticals. Gray encouraged her past the point of nagging and Diana finally agreed to make the appointment more to shut him up than because she had much hope that seeing yet another doctor would change anything.

At the beginning of her appointment, Dr. George asked why she had chosen this particular clinic and gave her a skeptical look when she said she'd read about it in an alternative health newsletter several years ago, but hadn't had time to make the trip while she was busy raising children.

"You live in Montana."

"Yes."

"And you have a family doctor there?"

"Yes, and he's a good doctor." Diana agreed. "But he isn't into alternative health care, or preventative medicine, and I am." Dr. George was still skeptical, seeming to be concerned mostly about her follow-up care. Diana never liked being told that she couldn't do something, but she was still a little surprised to hear herself assure him that she could make monthly trips to Seattle for follow-up care. He reluctantly agreed to take her as a patient.

• • •

The battery of tests Dr. George wanted made it necessary for Diana to spend a week in the area. She got a motel room with a kitchenette located within walking distance of the clinic. Each day she went to the clinic for whatever tests were on the agenda, and then she spent the rest of the day exploring the area. A fifteen minute walk in one direction brought her to a shopping area where she browsed through a variety of stores. The only thing she purchased was food to prepare in the kitchenette of her motel room. A twenty-minute walk in another direction brought her to another small shopping area which included her favorite type of retail establishment – a bookstore. While she was happily engrossed in searching for a new paperback book (or two) the time got away from her. It was twilight when she left the bookstore.

Trying not to panic, she walked as quickly as she could and was thankful that her motel was straight down the street she was on. True, it was about twenty blocks, and involved navigating over curbs, across streets, around flower pots, bus stop shelters, fire hydrants and other pedestrians, but on the bright side (pun intended) it was a main street with streetlights and traffic signals. It still took over an hour and was so stressful that when she finally unlocked her motel room, she fell into bed without changing into her pajamas or even fixing anything to eat. Lesson learned: pay attention to the time.

• • •

"On a scale of one to seven, with one being optimal health, and seven being in the hospital on life support, I would say that you are a five." The week of tests was completed, and in Dr. George's opinion, she was suffering from something he called adrenal exhaustion.

"What would a six be?" Diana asked, curiously, having already deduced that level eight would be dead.

"Level six would be the onset of some kind of degenerative disease." Dr. George replied, seriously. Diana digested that unwelcome medical opinion and knowing that degenerative diseases are those without cures, asked him what he recommended as a course of treatment.

"You need to drastically reduce the stress in your life." Dr. George said. Diana looked at him incredulously, but before she could respond, he continued. "That means rest as much as you can, and avoid as much stress as possible." He was quite serious. She reminded herself that she had consulted him, so she needed to keep an open mind about the treatment he recommended.

She went home, modified her diet, took her supplements, rested as much as was practical, and tried to avoid stress. Perhaps she had been right all those years ago, to associate her tiredness with an inability to handle stress. Within a few weeks, she was feeling a little bit better, and so she continued to see Dr. George and follow his advice throughout the winter and spring of the following year.

• • •

Diana had been seeing Dr. George for about a year when he referred her to the ophthalmologist who diagnosed her long-standing vision issues as Retinitis Pigmentosa, or RP. Looking out the window of the taxi after her appointment, she mentally reviewed the things Dr. Letz had told her.

Finally, her malady had a name. On the bright side, it was a relief to finally know that there was a reason for quite a few of the odd things that had happened in her life - things she had attributed to clumsiness, carelessness or stupidity. She wondered how much worse her vision would get, and hoped Dr. Letz was right and that she wouldn't go completely blind.

• • •

Diana and Jamie met in the fifth grade and though they had not lived in the same vicinity since junior high school, they were still close friends. Through the years, they stayed in touch via letters, phone calls, and more recently, e-mail. This evening, they sat in front of the gas fireplace in the family room, enjoying a glass of wine and the rare opportunity to visit face to face. Diana was spending the weekend at Jamie's house after her eye appointment and had just recounted her visit to Dr. Letz and his diagnosis of RP.

"I'm relieved to finally know what it is," Diana confided. "The things I've imagined were not good."

"What kinds of things did you imagine? "

"Brain damage, mini-strokes, neurological problems, insanity – you name it! You have to remember that I have a vivid imagination!" Diana joked.

"Are you worried about going blind?" Jamie asked as she sat in a glider chair with her feet on an ottoman. She had fair skin, short blond hair that framed her face and blue eyes which were, at that moment, regarding her oldest friend shrewdly.

"I haven't really had time to think about it. I knew something was wrong with my eyes, but I guess I didn't think in terms of not being able to fix it. And I didn't consider not being able to see at all. If I go blind, I'll have to deal with it. But to quote Dr. Letz, I'm not blind, yet."

"You know," Jamie looked thoughtful, "I think maybe your peripheral vision started to deteriorate way back in junior high."

"Why do you think that?" Diana asked, curiously. She always valued Jamie's opinion, so she settled back on the couch with her legs curled under her to listen.

"Sometimes you tripped over curbs and cracks in the sidewalk when we walked to and from school." Jamie replied. "You always laughed and said you were just clumsy, or not paying attention, but the thing is that you weren't clumsy in other circumstances. I mean, you were one of the more coordinated and athletic girls in our gym class."

"That would mean my symptoms showed up earlier than I thought – maybe around twelve, instead of sixteen." Diana said, thoughtfully. "You might be right, and it would explain quite a few other things too."

"Like what?"

"Like why I've never been good at girly things, like make-up and fingernail polish and putting together cute outfits. Why I can't remember faces. And maybe even why I fell asleep on the way home from just about every date I ever had."

"All the girly stuff would be hard if you can't see clearly." Jamie agreed. "You need to explain how falling asleep on dates ties in to your eyesight, though."

"Well, you've heard about people who were nearsighted and then once they got glasses they could actually see individual leaves on trees instead of a blob of green, and they suddenly realize that they never knew what they weren't seeing?" Jamie nodded. "If I always had night blindness, but didn't know it, then being out at night could have been so stressful that it was exhausting. Think about it – it was dark pretty much everywhere; at the movies, at dances, and in restaurants."

"I guess that makes sense." Jamie agreed.

"Now I suppose I'll have to be careful not to blame everything I can't do on my eyesight – or lack of eyesight." Diana quipped. She joked about it, but she was serious about not becoming a victim.

• • •

On the train ride back to Shelby, Diana's thoughts drifted back to another time in her life when she had decided it would be better to know exactly how bad things were instead of ignoring her problem. The knowledge had been a mixed blessing then, too.

She'd been in her thirties and aware that she had Pre-Menstrual Syndrome, but her symptoms were quite a bit different and much more severe than the ones described in her research, or discussed amongst her peers.

Her cycles were erratic, so instead of going on for a few days, her symptoms sometimes went on for weeks. Eventually her mood swings, irritability, and bizarre behavior caused her to wonder if she was, depending on the day, either in the process of losing her mind or already crazy. So she made an appointment with a psychologist. It would be better to know, she told herself firmly.

For a dozen sessions or so, she was as honest as she knew how to be while the therapist listened, asked questions and took notes. Finally, Dr. Rush offered her professional opinion.

"You are definitely not crazy." That was really good news and Diana was so glad to hear it from a trained professional that it took a minute for the bad news contained in the next sentence to register.

"You really don't need to continue to see me. I am convinced you do have severe PMS, and for that you need to consult a physician." The thought darted across Diana's mind that good news and bad news often seem to travel together.

She had come to think of her therapy sessions as time she spent in the eye of the hurricane, a brief respite where she could catch her breath and try to formulate strategies for dealing with the high winds and stormy seas that comprised the rest of her life at that time. As she drove home she knew she was really, really going to miss her visits with Dr. Rush. She also knew that she had no intention of consulting with a physician about her PMS. She had already, as the saying goes, "been there and done that".

In fact, she had consulted with quite a few physicians over the years, and none of those office visits had gone at all well or provided her with the answers she was seeking. Some had recommended that she take anti-depressants. Since they were the experts and she had consulted with them, she followed their advice and tried that, but it didn't help, and she thought being medicated added to her problems instead of alleviating them. Several physicians had given her the impression they thought she was a hypochondriac. None of them were un-professional enough to actually say that, but their skeptical looks spoke volumes. One doctor said that because she was a newlywed, her symptoms were probably caused by having too much sex. She was glad she had been speechless, because it was preferable to some of the things she might have said. She had not made any more appointments to see him. The one time she had consulted a woman physician, hoping for a higher level of understanding, the lady doctor had actually patted her hand in sympathy.

"Everyone gets a little tense before their period." She cooed, condescendingly.

So no, Diana knew she would not be consulting with any more physicians to help her cope with PMS. She saw no point in doing the same thing over and over again and expecting different results. It was

Nora who introduced her to the concept of alternative medicine and preventative health care, and who shared her sources for high quality supplements. With Nora's help, Diana changed her approach and spent the next decade doing her own research and reading everything she could find that mentioned PMS. She checked books out of the library and bought books from the bookstore. She subscribed to several alternative health newsletters and she experimented with diet, vitamins, herbal supplements, relaxation techniques, exercise, and anything else that offered hope of relieving her symptoms. She did telephone counseling with a PMS clinic whose number she found in a natural health newsletter, she located a source for and purchased progesterone cream and tried that. Some things worked and some things didn't, but she kept trying. On her worst days, she repeated her psychologist's words like a mantra, chanting under her breath.

"I am not crazy. I am not crazy. I am not crazy."

• • •

As the train rolled on through the darkness on the overnight journey towards home, Diana's thoughts turned to the present. Once again she found herself with a condition that didn't fall into normal parameters. With PMS that had been a bad thing, but it sounded like this time, with RP, it was an excellent thing. She was sure it would turn out to be a mixed blessing, because being odd meant that she would be charting new territory, unable to rely on research or protocol. But she had done that before, and she had a new mantra to focus on when she got frustrated.

"I am not blind! I am not blind! I am not blind!"

• • •

It took a few weeks for the RP diagnosis to soak into Diana's reality. As she pondered some of the events from her past through the prism of new understanding, another phrase from Dr. Letz echoed through her memory.

"Most people who have RP are legally blind by the time they are in their thirties."

For once, she was very happy not to be most people. In this context, being different was indeed, as Kermit the Frog sang, "Beautiful!"

There had been other times when Diana had not enjoyed being different, like when she was eight years old and her mom died. She hadn't known a mom could die, and after hers did, she didn't know any other children to whom such a thing had happened. She had no point of reference to see if how she was feeling was normal or not.

The day her mom died was the first defining moment in her life, forever separating her life into sections she thought of as "before" and "after". Her whole family had to start over. Familiar things disappeared and were replaced by the unknown; house, school, neighborhood, friends, and teachers. She had moved through life in a fog of grief and uncertainty for a long, long time.

She suspected she was in the middle of another of life's defining moments with this diagnosis of RP. It wasn't a choice she had made, like whether or not to go to college, whom to marry or how to parent her children. It was something she hadn't chosen and couldn't change; she could only adjust. The plaque hanging on her kitchen wall summed it up pretty clearly. *"It is what it is, but it will become what you make it."* She vowed that she would be the one to adjust rather than to expect the rest of the world to make allowances for her problem.

CHAPTER 6

Knowledge Is Power

· · ·

DIANA BEGAN TO RESEARCH RETINITIS Pigmentosa, amazed at how much easier research was on the internet than it had been at the library. At the same time, she was disappointed to learn how little information was available other than what Dr. Letz had already told her.

Dr. Letz said that RP was hereditary. Diana thought that was odd. One of her cousins had lost most of her eyesight as a complication of diabetes, but not a single one of her other relatives including grandparents, parents, siblings, aunts, uncles and cousins, had displayed any of the symptoms of RP. Neither did her children. If there was a blessing in not having a definite diagnosis until this point in her life, she thought it was that all of her children were well past the usual age when RP symptoms appeared, and she hadn't worried about their vision other than making sure they had regular eye exams. Sometimes, ignorance really was bliss!

Though she did have trouble differentiating between navy and black or dark brown and black, she did not consider herself to be color blind. She had decided it would be a good idea to focus on the good things and try to minimize the not so good things, and so she counted not being color blind among her blessings.

Night blindness was her most familiar symptom. She knew by experience that the term also defined being unable to see clearly in dim light of any kind, including most indoor spaces like other people's homes, airports and airplanes, stores, churches, and restaurants.

• • •

Diana had always assumed that decorating was one of those girly things she was not good at. An afghan artfully draped over a rocking chair, a basket of silk flowers on the bottom stair, potted plants, assorted candles, knick-knacks and pictures arranged on tables and shelves. All were pleasing to both the eye and the spirit, but they also made her nervous. She had tripped over an umbrella holder in Jamie's entryway, and she still cringed remembering the potted plant she'd accidently knocked off the coffee table at Lynn's apartment. Thank goodness the pot didn't break, but there was potting soil all over the floor. The worst part of any spill was that she was completely capable of causing a bigger problem if she tried to help clean up, so other people ended up cleaning up after her.

• • •

Diana always turned on her reading light in an airplane so that she could see her immediate surroundings as well as whatever she was reading when they turned out the main cabin lights. And she always went to the bathroom in the airport before boarding. Except for the time she didn't, and halfway through the flight, she really needed to use the restroom. They were sitting in the seventeenth row. Gray looked skeptical and asked if she could go by herself. Truthfully she wasn't sure, but she was certainly going to try. With one hand on the luggage compartments overhead (a trick she had learned by watching airline personnel in turbulent conditions) and her eyes on the lights at the front of the plane, she felt her way towards the front of the airplane, murmuring "sorry" and "excuse me" as she bumped into the arms and shoulders of people who were leaning out into the aisle. She didn't blame them for using the aisle space because the seats were cramped, but she also didn't feel too badly about brushing against them. She had planned to count the seats when she made her return trip down the aisle, again with one hand brushing along the luggage compartment overhead, but since she couldn't see them that strategy didn't work very well. Remembering her experience in the movie theatre, she didn't dare count by touching the seat backs on the way by, for fear her hand would land on someone's shoulder instead. The reading lights that were on blinded her so she couldn't even tell whether the seat they were shining on was empty or occupied. Why oh why had she ordered that Coke in the terminal, she wondered irritably, as she inched her way down the aisle. As if he were psychic, Gray stepped into the aisle so she could see him. Two more steps and she slid past him into the window seat. He must get pretty tired of watching out for her, she thought.

• • •

"I called last week to wish you a happy birthday" Jamie said when Diana answered the phone. "Gray told me you were spending the week at Flathead Lake." She paused. "As a counselor at church camp! How did that happen?" Diana explained how Cole & Riley were scheduled to be counselors and that the camp director called two days before they were to report and said he was afraid they would have to cancel the whole camp. Apparently the female counselors he had lined up couldn't make it and he couldn't have camp without them.

"So you volunteered?" Jamie asked.

"Not exactly! First I tried to think of someone else, but I couldn't come up with anyone who was good with that age group and also able to drop everything and go at the last minute. Then the director said he needed just one more counselor because a woman from his church had said she'd help. I hated to see all the kids disappointed because of two irresponsible college girls. I knew Gray wouldn't mind, and my kids were going to be there anyway, so I said I'd do it."

"Sounds like the camp director was pretty sure you would volunteer." Jamie commented and Diana readily agreed that she had been set up, but since it was for a good cause, she didn't mind very much.

"How did it go?"

"The other woman and I weren't responsible for any of the lessons or activities; we were mainly there to chaperone in the girls' cabins at night. I really liked the camp setting and I'm good with middle school kids, so it was pretty easy, really."

"But something is bothering you." Jamie probed. So Diana confessed that each day concluded with a campfire at an area called Inspiration Point, and that she hadn't even thought about leading her girls back to their cabin afterwards – in the dark on a path through the trees -- until the campfire was over that first night.

"Oh! What happened?"

"I was just starting to panic when Riley showed up beside me. The girls in my group were all gathered around and he casually asked them to lead the way towards the cabin and said we would come last and do a head count when we got there."

"So did you take a flashlight the next night?" There was a long silence and when Diana finally spoke she just said it was complicated.

"Try to explain because I want to understand." Jamie encouraged.

"Flashlights don't work for me. They don't illuminate enough area and they are not bright enough. On an uneven dirt trail through bushes and trees - a spotlight might work, but I doubt it, because it would still have to be focused either on the trail or on the way ahead. I need both of those areas lit up at the same time so my eyes don't have to constantly re-focus from light to dark."

"Oh!" Jamie said. "How did Riley help you?"

"He gave me a flashlight to shine on the ground and then walked behind me with his hands on my shoulders gave me directions while he guided me. All I had to focus on was the path." Diana explained. "Cole and Riley were co-counselors, so every night Riley helped me get to our cabin while Cole supervised their group of kids."

"I'm glad your sons were there and it worked out, then." Jamie said.

"Yeah – of course it is one more item on the list of things I can't do by myself anymore." Diana groused.

"But on the bright side, since you've never been a camp counselor before, you probably won't miss it!" Jamie laughed.

• • •

One Sunday as they prepared to receive communion Diana asked Gray to go ahead of her. He always stood back to let her, or any woman for that matter, go ahead of him, so he raised an eyebrow at her request. When she whispered that she wanted to walk behind his light colored shirt, he got it right away and stepped in front of her, holding his right hand out behind him so she could curl the fingers of her right hand into his.

In the Methodist church, the communion bread is dipped into the wine or juice. At one time each person tore their own piece of communion bread from the loaf. Diana had been grateful when that procedure changed and the servers began to tear a piece of bread from the loaf and hand it to each person instead. She was always very careful when she dipped her bread; afraid she might inadvertently hit the edge of the cup with her hand and knock it to the floor. The brown pottery goblet was hard for her to see clearly, especially if the communion server wore dark colored clothing, and most of them did.

Their communion routine had been working beautifully for quite awhile and then one Sunday when they reached the head of the line, instead of the usual half loaf of white bread, the communion server held a brown pottery plate heaped with neatly cut cubes of dense dark brown bread. Diana hadn't been expecting that. Straining her eyes to see the brown bread on the brown plate, she picked up one piece from the edge of the pile, and as she attempted to dip it, dropped it into the cup. Her second attempt was successful, but she followed Gray back to their seat, feeling clumsy and inept. So much for the spiritual aspects of the sacrament of communion, she thought.

• • •

After dinner in a crowded restaurant, Riley walked behind her with his hands on her shoulders, guiding her between tables and around people with gentle pressure and verbal clues. When they got to the door, the perky young hostess who had seated them held the door open.

"Oh, have we had too much to drink?" she cooed sympathetically. Diana hesitated, wondering if it would be worth it to try and explain. Apparently she and Riley simultaneously came to the same conclusion.

"Keep walking. She doesn't mean to be rude and it's too crowded to stop and explain." Riley murmured. "And anyway, she's kind of cute."

• • •

"Sorry that took so long," Diana apologized. "There was a line, as usual." She and Gray were attending a college football game and the restrooms were located underneath the stadium where the lighting ranged from dim to non-existent. Gray had walked with her and pointed out the door of the ladies room, then waited to help her navigate back to their seats. As always when she was faced with something she could not do without assistance, she was simultaneously grateful and resentful.

"Hopefully I haven't been reported to security as a pervert for hanging around outside the women's restroom." Gray joked, and laughing about that took her mind off how irritating it was that at her age -- she needed to be taken to the bathroom.

• • •

Narrowing peripheral vision was a symptom that had sneaked up on Diana. It was more than being unable to see things off to the side. It also referred to things in the upper and lower areas of vision. Diana could never tell if people reached out to shake her hand, and that included not only meeting new people, but also receiving lines at weddings and funerals and the passing of the peace in church. She tripped over curbs, wet floor signs, towed luggage, and cracks in the sidewalk. She ran into low tree branches, hanging flower baskets, guy wires, signposts and doorways. She didn't see other people's grocery carts, splashed through mud puddles, and once she ran knee-cap first into a cement bench as she and Gray walked from their airplane into the terminal. She still didn't know why there were benches, cement or otherwise, in the walk-way between the terminal and the airplane, but maybe people needed to stop and rest on the journey between plane and terminal, or between terminal and plane. Whatever.

• • •

Coming out of church one Sunday, Gray grabbed the back of Diana's sweater in a choke hold, just in time to keep her from bowling over a woman who had bent over to retrieve something off the floor. When Diana got over her irritation at being so unceremoniously grabbed, and by the throat, no less, she was grateful for Gray's quick reflexes. Had he not been there, she probably would have run into and then fallen on top of that elderly woman.

• • •

As for gaps in her vision field, Dr. Letz had told her to think of her vision field as being made up of pixels like those in a digital photograph and then to imagine that she had some of her pixels missing. It was good to finally understand the reason that she could not see things she'd dropped or laid down, or finer details of the bigger picture, including recognizing people's faces.

He had explained that the brain fills in those holes, or missing pixels, according to the background. She had no idea how big those areas of missing pixels were, so she wasn't really sure how much of what she saw was real and how much her brain filled in for her. That made it difficult to explain the vision gaps to other people. So unless they asked specific questions, she didn't bother. She wasn't trying to hide her disability; she just did not want her disability to become the focus of her life.

Diana was grateful that her brain was able to fill in those vision gaps, because it sounded like the alternative would be Swiss cheese vision. She certainly did not wish for big black areas in her vision; but at the same time, it was frustrating to be constantly losing track of kitchen utensils while cooking, or garden tools while doing yard work. It was annoying to spill, break or bump into things. She could look right at something and not see it. Then if one corner of whatever she was not seeing found its way out of an area of missing pixels and into an area of healthy pixels, her brain would fill in the rest and like magic – poof! There it was!

• • •

Sometimes, when Diana asked for assistance in the grocery store, the item she wanted was right where she had been looking. Now and then the packaging had changed so she didn't recognize it, but more often it was exactly where it should have been with a familiar package and logo, and she just didn't see it. She learned to ignore or laugh off the funny looks she got from store employees and other shoppers.

"I can't find it. That doesn't mean it isn't there, it just means I didn't see it." She'd say with a smile and a shake of her head. Some days Diana was sure that her brain cells were all so busy helping her to see that there were none left with which to think. It was certainly one explanation for her frequent brain fog!

• • •

The alarm went off as Diana walked through the metal detector and she realized that she still had her cell phone in her pocket. She and Gray flew fairly often, and she knew better, but there were quite a few things to remember about airport security, and the procedures weren't exactly the same at every airport, making it easy to forget something. In some airports, TSA agents wanted everything placed in a plastic bin and in others they wanted shoes or backpacks placed directly on the conveyor belt. She sighed as she turned back, removed her phone from her pocket and placed it into the dish offered by the TSA agent, then turned towards the metal detector to try again.

"Ma'am, you've been randomly selected..." she didn't even listen to the rest of the spiel from the voice behind her. This happened often enough that she believed she was being targeted.

"...If you could step over here, please." In the dim light, Diana could just make out the blur of a face where she knew the voice was coming from, and she spoke to that blur as politely as she could manage.

"I'm sorry, but I can't see where you are pointing. It would helpful if you could tell me how many steps, and which direction – forward, left, or right." It wasn't this person's fault she couldn't see very well in this dimly lit area, and she reminded herself that he was just doing his job. Her personal opinion that his job was an unnecessary one that harassed innocent, law-abiding passengers without doing a single thing to prevent terrorism was completely beside the point.

"Ma'am? Are you visually impaired?" The voice was in front of her now and she could see his face, though his features were still blurry.

"Yes."

72

"Can you see my hand?" Diana looked down and was mildly surprised that she actually could see his hand. It was encased in a pale blue latex glove, and showed up pretty well against the gray of the floor. She nodded and said yes again.

"Take my hand, please." She complied and he led her back to the metal detector, without performing the extra screening for which she had been "randomly" selected.

"She's visually impaired." He explained to his counterpart on the other side of the metal detector, who responded with the usual hand gesture and an added verbal direction for her to walk straight ahead. She pulled her elbows in and kept her hands in front of her to avoid touching the sides. She would never forget the time she set off the alarm because she automatically trailed her fingers along the side of the metal detector like she did when she walked near a wall. Talk about embarrassing! This time no bells went off and she was able to retrieve her belongings, put her jacket and her shoes back on and look around for Gray.

As they waited in the boarding area, she pondered what had just happened. Her theory that the reason she was often selected for "random" extra screening was because TSA agents picked up on her elevated stress level had just been validated. Although annoying to her, it was an indication that they were observant and well trained, and she tried to be grateful for that, at least.

Today, she had admitted to being "visually impaired" and the use of the term had helped her to avoid that extra screening. It was more than a little bit tempting to proclaim herself as a VIP next time she traveled, but she already knew she wouldn't do it.

Years before Diana was aware of her own vision issues, she had noticed a gray haired woman wearing a backpack and tapping the floor ahead of her with a white cane as she made her way through the crowded Seattle airport. She was surrounded by a six foot band of space because the other travelers, even as they hurried to and from their own flights, noticed that white cane and made allowances for her disability. Diana had remembered that blind woman several times since she discovered that she had RP, especially since she also had gray hair and carried a backpack. That blind woman always came to mind when someone asked Diana why she didn't have a white cane or somehow let people know of her disability.

"What would people think if they saw me with a white cane, and then I pulled out my kindle and started reading?" she asked. She had long ago stopped caring what people thought of her personally, that wasn't the point. The point was that she did not want to appear to be faking a disability in order to get special privileges. She would admit to being visually handicapped if someone asked her, but she wasn't going to use it as a crutch – even if it was a way to avoid those "random" extra screenings.

• • •

Riley had been to Cancun for a wedding and while he was there he bought Diana a new tote bag for her birthday. She always enjoyed presents, and was as touched by gifts from her adult sons as she had been with the gifts they gave her when they were children. Tote bags are all similar, and this one was no exception. It had handles and two zippered compartments, and was purple with "Cancun" lettered in beige on the outside. She noticed and commented on the light cream colored interior as soon she opened it and Riley told her he had been to several vendors and unzipped a multitude of tote bags until he found one that was not black on the inside. The mental picture of him being thoughtful enough to inspect tote bag interiors made her smile. Little things mean a lot.

• • •

Hiking was a family activity, partly because they lived so close to Glacier National Park. As newlyweds, Gray and Diana had hiked by themselves, or with friends or family. When the children were small, Gray often carried two children when they got tired of walking; one piggy-back and another astride his shoulders. As the kids got older, they ran ahead on the trail engaged in fierce competition to see who could get to the top first. There had been a few years when their teen-aged sons didn't want to hike with them at all, but as adults and then married adults with children, hiking had again become a family activity.

Gray loved to hike, but as she got older, Diana noticed that she enjoyed it less each time she went. She fell often enough that she began hiking more slowly. In an effort to watch where she was going, she spent more time looking at the trail than at the scenery. She complained that Gray hiked too fast. He couldn't seem to slow down, so he tried hiking behind her so he wouldn't get too far ahead, and then she complained that he was crowding her and breathing down her neck. Gray thought she wasn't as physically fit as she had been when she was younger, and she thought he might be right. Or maybe she hoped that was the reason she had trouble.

One summer when Jamie, Mitch, and their daughter Mia came to visit, the three women left Mitch to fend for himself while they spent an afternoon hiking. Diana expected it to be a good experience without any impatient men along to cramp her style. But she stumbled several times, fell twice, and actually had trouble discerning where the path was a couple of times. When Jamie asked if something was wrong, she said she'd gotten new glasses and was still adjusting to the bifocal lenses. She did have new glasses, and they had bifocal lenses, so it wasn't a lie, exactly.

It was the next year, after her RP diagnosis when Diana realized that the combination of her lack of peripheral vision and her inability to see in dim light was what made hiking so difficult. Having identified the problem, she thought she could compensate by paying closer attention to the trail. She knew she would still have to hike at a slower pace and probably miss a lot of scenery because she couldn't look around unless she stopped walking, but it was worth doing. She had moderate success with this strategy when the hike was in the open, like from Logan Pass to Granite Park Chalet, for instance. Hiking through the trees, though, turned out to be a whole different problem. Walking from sunlight to shade and then back to sunlight didn't give her eyes time to adjust and she saw either shadows or glare.

• • •

Avalanche Lake is one of the most popular hikes in Glacier Park, and had always been one of Diana's personal favorites, maybe because she'd hiked it so often over the years. It was an easy two mile climb with a lake at the top where they always took a break and had a snack before hiking back down. In all the years they had hiked this trail, only once had they witnessed the event which gave the lake its name.

It happened on Memorial Day Weekend, on one of those spring days when the sky was blue and the sun was bright and warm, but the air was still cool. Their family was nearing the top when they heard thunder, and Diana hoped they still had garbage bags in the bottom of the backpack that contained their lunch, because garbage bags made great emergency ponchos. They hadn't expected rain today, but weather could change and it was good to be prepared. They were all puzzled when they heard another clap of thunder as they sat beside the lake munching their sandwiches and enjoying the scenery. How could there be thunder when there wasn't a cloud in the sky? Suddenly Gray pointed across the lake at the mountains.

"Look!" he exclaimed, and they watched in awe as an avalanche of snow tumbled silently down the mountain mere seconds before they heard the roar of sound -- just like thunder.

• • •

One summer during a family reunion, a group of relatives decided to hike to Avalanche Lake. Knowing that the hike went through the trees, Diana took her kindle and planned to wait for them at the car. Her nieces and nephew wouldn't hear of it, and promised to help her. She rationalized that she had survived the last time and could probably manage once more, and so she agreed to the hike.

True to their word, Eileen and Nick hiked with her, alerting her to rocks, tree roots and mud puddles along the way and lending her an arm or a hand when she needed it for balance. It was a successful hike because Diana didn't fall, not even once, and she thoroughly enjoyed the companionship of her family. Then, on the way back down the mountain, not one, not two, but three different times, other hikers stopped and offered their assistance.

"Oh thank you, but I'm fine, I'm just slow." Diana assured each of them with a laugh. By the third time, her laugh sounded a bit strained even to her own ears. The last guy who stopped to offer assistance said he could carry her down the mountain if she needed him to do so! Diana sincerely hoped he was out of earshot before she got the giggles at the mental picture of an old lady getting a piggyback ride.

When she stopped laughing, Diana decided two things. The first was that the majority of people you meet along the paths of life are generous, caring, helpful individuals. And the second was that hiking was another activity she probably wouldn't do anymore, because it exhausted her and was too much trouble for other people.

CHAPTER 7

Crash!

• • •

DIANA WAS UNDER THE IMPRESSION that the gaps in her vision were fairly small. She didn't know where she got that idea, because Dr. Letz had not said that. She supposed there was no way to measure them since the brain was so busy trying to fill them in. She assumed that their size didn't matter because she had learned to compensate for them.

Then one day as she was making a right hand turn onto Main Street, she hit a pedestrian. Not just any pedestrian, mind you, but an elderly man, using a walker, in a crosswalk. She felt the bump, stopped the car and jumped out. The man was sprawled in the crosswalk, his walker tipped over beside him, one of the wheels still spinning. The fact that there was no blood, and that the man was conscious didn't do much to remove the horror of living in the middle of her worst nightmare.

"Oh, my God, I'm so sorry. Are you okay?" she gasped.

"Yeah, I'm fine. It was just a little bump. Help me up, would you?" he grumbled.

"I think we'd better wait to make sure you're okay," Diana said, and then she ran to her car, unlocked the trunk and brought a stadium cushion for his head and a blanket to cover him.

The man's son owned the store on the opposite corner and had witnessed the accident. He had already called the ambulance and the police, and was crouched beside his dad, asking him questions. His wife walked over to where Diana sat in her car, shaking like a leaf, horrified at what had happened.

"I know you feel terrible about this," the woman said, "but it may turn out to be a blessing. This accident may even save his life." Diana stared at her, completely speechless, and the woman hastened to explain.

"You see, we've been trying to get him in to the doctor for a check-up, but he refused. Now he'll have to go – he'll have no choice."

Just then, the police and ambulance arrived, so Diana was spared having to make a reply. That was a good thing, because she could not think of a single thing to say. At that particular moment in time, she didn't feel like a blessing to anyone.

After the man was transported to the hospital, the deputy asked Diana to drive to the sheriff's office to fill out the accident report. About the last thing she wanted to do was drive anywhere, but some-times there is no choice and the next thing simply must be done, so she got back into the car and did as the deputy had asked. At the sheriff's office, Diana stared blankly at the pieces of paper on the table in front of her, and the deputy had to repeat himself several times as he explained what she needed to do. Her brain felt like mush, her fingers had trouble holding onto the pen, and it took a long time for her to fill out the forms.

"It appears to be an accident." The deputy said, kindly. "Sometimes accidents happened."

"I hit a pedestrian with my car," Diana said, as if saying it would alleviate some of the horror. It didn't.

When the forms were finally completed and Diana was free to go, she got into the car again, and drove directly to her insurance agent's office to report the accident to them. Then she drove to Gray's office, walked in and sat down in front of his desk. She waited until he looked up before she spoke.

"I just hit a pedestrian with my car." She said. "The ambulance took him to the hospital. I think he's okay. I filled out the police report and notified the insurance company."

Before Gray had a chance to say anything, Diana stood up, walked out the door, and got back into the car. Slowly and carefully, she drove home and parked the car in the garage, wondering vaguely if she was in shock. She decided she probably was.

When Gray got home from work about an hour later, he asked her what happened.

"I just didn't see him." She replied, and Gray did not say another word. All three of her sons called as soon as they heard. She told them she didn't hit the guy hard enough to cause any damage to her or the car, and each of them assured her they were worried about her mental and emotional state, not her physical condition, and certainly not the car.

"Oh, I'm fine," She insisted.

"Every vehicle has blind spots." A friend commented.

"Accidents happen." Her neighbor said.

"Something like that could happen to anyone." A total stranger assured her. But it hadn't happened to anyone, it had happened to her, and it wasn't the first time. Well, it was the first and hopefully the last time she hit a pedestrian, but it wasn't her first accident.

The next day Diana learned that the man was in the hospital with a broken leg and his blood tests confirmed that he did need some other medications. So his daughter-in-law had been right, but Diana knew that she'd never be able to believe that running into him with her car was a blessing.

On the front page of the next issue of the weekly newspaper, in living color above the fold, was a picture of Diana's car in the middle of the intersection with the EMTs loading the injured man into the ambulance. Under the picture was a write-up of the accident, so everyone in town knew what had happened and many of them asked how she was doing. She assured them all that she was fine but of course she wasn't fine. For weeks afterwards, she didn't sleep well. When she did sleep, she had nightmares about the accident, waking suddenly in a cold sweat with her heart pounding, then unable to get back to sleep.

Diana had heard, and even laughed at, the joke about how you get more points if you run over someone who is using a walker, especially on the sidewalk or in a crosswalk. Now she had two words for that joke. "Not Funny!"

• • •

Diana believed in facing up to and conquering her fears and phobias, and it seemed as if she had been doing that throughout her life. Whether she had more than the usual number of fears and phobias, she didn't know. She had nearly drowned as a child, and as a result had been terrified of the water during the rest of her childhood. Even so, she learned to water-ski as a teenager. She always buckled her life jacket securely first, and she closed her eyes, gritted her teeth and focused on breathing as the rope tightened and the boat accelerated. But she learned, and other than a few heart-stopping moments just as the boat pulled her out of the water, she enjoyed it. In college, she enrolled in and completed every swimming class that was offered, starting with basic swimming and progressing through lifeguard training. She still didn't love to swim, but instead of being terrified around the water, she was just tense. She enrolled her children in swimming lessons as soon as they were old enough, and saw to it that they had lessons every summer. When her husband bought a boat, she helped teach their kids how to water-ski. She counted it a personal victory that they were all proficient swimmers who enjoyed water sports.

She also had a fear of all things medical. If one reads much psychology, and Diana was a voracious reader, every problem in adulthood seemed to be caused by some childhood trauma. Her family told stories of the hysterical crying fits she had thrown whenever she needed an immunization, and she also had her tonsils removed before she started school, so it was possible that she had some kind of real or imagined trauma in her past. At any rate, the antiseptic smells of clinics or hospitals made her nauseous and light headed, she could not stand the sight of blood and was deathly afraid of needles. Being pregnant and having children had helped her get over most of that.

She had fallen out of trees and off her bicycle, been tossed from the backs of horses a time or two, and taken many a tumble while participating in sports. All of which gave her plenty of experience with getting up, dusting herself off and trying again. She thought this would be another one of those times when she had to get up and try again, but there was just no comparison between risking sore muscles, skinned knees, or a bruised ego, and the mind numbing terror that she might hit another pedestrian. She told herself it was understandable that she should be nervous and that it would pass. But it didn't. If anything, it got worse, because the thought that wouldn't stay in the back of her mind was that in addition to the actual accidents she'd had, there were several near misses. Like the time she'd made a left turn and a semi had blasted its horn at her. She hadn't even seen him, and although there were no screeching brakes, she knew it had been too close. Or the several times she'd signaled to change lanes and been honked at by a car that she hadn't seen. She always attributed those either to the other driver, or to that ever-elusive blind spot, making it the car's fault instead of hers. Then there was that snow-drift she'd buried her dad's car in so many years ago. Any one of those situations could have ended badly.

● ● ●

Diana could feel the tension in her neck and shoulders and knew she would have a headache later. In the two years since her accident, she had come to hate driving. Lately, she had been thinking about all the ways her life would change if, or more accurately, when, she stopped driving. As it was she only drove in good weather and in the middle of the day, and she was very, very careful. She knew she was rationalizing because she was reluctant to give up the freedom and independence driving afforded her, even though driving was getting more and more stressful.

On this particular occasion, her fingers were clamped around the steering wheel of her sporty red Cadillac ETC as she drove the twenty-two miles from Shelby to the dealership in Cut Bank for an oil change and some routine maintenance. She never turned the radio on when she drove, afraid that it would distract her. She shuddered remembering her younger days when she had routinely disobeyed the posted speed limit. These days she always drove the speed limit – or less. She checked and re-checked her mirrors, and didn't see any cars on the long straight stretch of highway behind her. She seemed to be the only car on the road. Mere seconds later, she was startled by a car zooming past her. She had been traveling just under the speed limit; the car that passed her seemed to be going quite a bit faster but she still thought she should have seen it coming when she checked her mirrors. Her heart rate, already accelerated from the shock of the car passing her, sped up even more as she realized that she had never thought about the gaps in her vision field in the context of the mirrors on her car. That led her to consider the possibility that she if didn't see things in her rear view mirror, was she able to see oncoming traffic? She realized she had no idea, really, and resolved never to pass another car, just in case.

While she sat in the lobby of the dealership waiting for the car to be serviced and dreading the drive home, she made up her mind. Today, she was going to hang up her car keys. Forever!

"That's it." She told Gray that evening after she explained what had happened that day. "I'm not going to drive anymore."

From that day forward, Diana wore a backpack and walked around Shelby to do her errands. She told herself that the exercise was good for her. Shelby was small enough that she could walk anywhere she needed to go in thirty minutes or less, and she carried her cell phone with her, so in an emergency or bad weather, she could call someone for a ride. She also carried her identification with her, just in case. Neither Gray nor her sons questioned her decision. In fact, Diana got the impression the kids, at least, were relieved that she was no longer driving.

CHAPTER 8

Adventures And Mis-Adventures

• • •

Diana made several trips to Seattle for doctor appointments with Dr. George, the NRT practitioner, and for regular eye exams with Dr. Letz. As a mode of travel, her choices were to take a commercial flight or to ride the train. Flying was faster, until you took into consideration that the nearest airport was in Great Falls, and the flight left early in the morning and returned late at night. That meant an earlier morning and a later night for whoever took her to meet the plane and returned to pick her up. Even if she stayed in a motel on one or both ends of the trip, which added to the time and expense of the trip, someone had to transport her to and from Great Falls, a one hundred and eighty mile round trip.

Diana opted to ride the train. Amtrak took seventeen hours to get to Seattle, but the westbound train stopped in Shelby in the late afternoon and the eastbound train arrived just before noon. She packed an overnight bag, snacks, a bottle of water, a blanket, and something to read, and depending on how her appointments were scheduled, she stayed one or two nights in a motel and used taxi cabs or town car services for her transportation needs.

In another few years, GPS would be standard equipment in taxi cabs and on personal cell phones, but at that time, such was not the case, so Diana always took the precaution of printing a map and driving directions from Google Maps just so she knew where the taxi drivers were supposed to take her. And it isn't true that men never ask for directions. One of the town car drivers was thrilled that she had a map he could use, because he didn't know how to get where she needed to go. He assured her that he would have found it eventually, but having the map made everything easier.

The lower level section of Amtrak's passenger train is reserved for senior citizens and those with handicaps, and Diana always booked her seat there. The larger windows let in more light, the aisles were wider, there were no stairs to navigate, and it was close to the bathroom.

She remembered one summer when her grandparents had ridden the train from California to Montana to visit her. They were in their eighties at the time, and it was hard for them, especially her grandmother, to get up and down the stairs to the restrooms on the lower level of the train. The train swayed from side to side as it clacked along the tracks, and the U-shaped stairwell was narrow and dark. Diana suggested that they change their seats to the lower level for the return trip, and her grandmother had been highly insulted, insisting that neither of them were handicapped.

It was one of the first times Diana thought about aging with the realization that she would be old one day, and she resolved to make adjustments along the way, not only for her own sake, but also for the sake of the people who might worry about her.

Diana remembered that resolution to age gracefully some fifteen years later when she had to put her dad in a nursing home. It was nearly as traumatic for her as it was for him, because he didn't want to go, and she hated that there was no other option. She had medical evaluations, a psychological recommendation, and her sister's experience as a full-time caregiver, but it still came down to her decision as the custodial child and it was both difficult and heart-breaking.

"When I need twenty-four hour care, and that day comes to every-one at some point, don't feel guilty. Just get me a room in the nursing home, and go on with your lives." Diana told her children. She was completely serious, but since they had all inherited her sarcasm and dry wit, they asked if next week would work for her.

• • •

One afternoon, Diana boarded the westbound train and stepped to one side just inside the door. Suddenly, she was accosted by a demanding voice out of the semi-darkness.

"What are you doing in here?"

"I'm waiting for my eyes to adjust before I find a seat." She re-plied. She had barely finished speaking, when the voice fired another question.

"Does your ticket say 'lower level'?" Diana replied that it did.

"This section is reserved for seniors––you aren't old enough!" The rude disembodied voice asserted.

"Thank you," Diana replied, and then added politely, "I believe it is also reserved for people with handicaps and disabilities."

"You don't look handicapped!" the voice snapped.

"Well, handicaps aren't always visible, are they?" Diana commented mildly. She didn't really mind talking about her vision issues, but it gave her a great deal of satisfaction to thwart this woman just because she was so rude. Perhaps realizing she'd come on rather strongly, the woman whom Diana now thought of as the 'High Inquisitor' asked her next question in a slightly more pleasant tone.

"Where are you going?"

"Seattle." Diana said.

"So is she," the woman said as she gestured with a thumb over her shoulder, indicating the back of the car. Diana's eyes had partially adjusted by this time, and she could just make out a short, gray haired woman in a red sweat suit standing at the far end of the car. It looked like she was taking the opportunity to stretch while the train was at a standstill. The three of them appeared to be the only occupants in this car. Wondering how long she and the lady in red would have to put up with the High Inquisitor, Diana turned her attention back towards her interrogator, now able to see that she was short and stocky, dressed in black pants and a bulky maroon turtleneck sweater. Her spiky black hair looked dyed and she wore a lot of make-up. Her black glasses had square rims and she kept pushing them up on her nose. Diana couldn't tell her age, but from the querulous quality of her voice guessed she fit the senior citizen guideline for lower level seating.

"Where are you heading, if you don't mind my asking?" Diana asked politely.

"Vancouver," the woman replied, grudgingly, as if she did mind. Perhaps it was okay for her to grill others about their itinerary, but not okay for anyone to inquire as to the details of her trip.

"Oh." Diana paused and then asked, curiously. "Do you mean Vancouver, British Columbia--or Vancouver, Washington?"

"Vancouver, Washington." The reply was delivered in a tone of voice suggesting that Diana was an idiot for asking.

"I see." Diana said. "Well in that case, either you, or the two of us, are in the wrong car." She gestured to the woman in red as she spoke. Diana was not an expert in geography, but she had been on this train several times and was pretty sure that she and the lady in red wouldn't be traveling with the High Inquisitor. She tried not to let her relief show.

"What do you mean?" the woman demanded.

"This train separates in Spokane in the middle of the night. Part of it goes on to Seattle, and the other part goes to Portland. So if you are in the wrong car, you could end up someplace you weren't planning to go." The black haired woman stared at her, speechless.

"Vancouver, Washington is just across the river from Portland, Oregon, so I think you need to be in the part of the train that goes to Portland, instead of the section going to Seattle." When Diana finished her explanation, the woman stomped off without a reply, presumably in search of a train official.

Diana got settled across the aisle from the woman in the red sweats, A few minutes later, an Amtrak employee appeared, took two bags from the storage area beside the door, and left again. He returned just as the train pulled out of the station and updated them, totally failing to contain a wide grin.

"The Portland car is packed and this car's former troublemaker is now jammed into a window seat next to a very large, very loud woman with dreadlocks and an attitude."

"Karma – gotta love it!" Diana thought to herself as she exchanged a look and a smile with the lady in the red sweats.

• • •

As she had done several times, Diana was spending the night in a motel near the airport in Great Falls in preparation for an early morning flight to California the next day. She made this trip every other month to spend time with her terminally ill sister. It was so hard to see the ravages of the disease each time she visited. It was also a blessing to be able to spend time with Marcy and do what she could to help. Marcy's children had rallied around her, of course. But there were a few things Marcy didn't want to ask of them, or discuss with them.

"We're all going to die someday." Marcy said. "I just have a pretty good idea when and how." Diana was amazed at and inspired by her younger sister's courage.

Usually Gray brought her to Great Falls and they went out to dinner before he left her at the motel and returned home. This time she saved him a trip by catching a ride with someone who was driving through Great Falls on their way to Helena. She had arrived mid-afternoon and was unable to face so many hours in a motel room by herself, so she spent the afternoon browsing in the craft store and the book store across the parking lot from her motel. There was a theatre at the opposite end of the shopping area, where "Harry Potter and the Goblet of Fire" was playing. She had been looking for an opportunity to see the latest Harry Potter movie, and hoping a movie would take her mind away from somber thoughts about her sister, she decided to attend the seven o'clock showing.

She walked to the theatre without a problem, but once her ticket was purchased, she had to use every trick in her repertoire to find her seat in the crowded theatre. She trailed her hand lightly along the wall, felt for the steps with her toe, and watched the floor to see the shoes of other people. She had discovered that shoes, especially athletic shoes that had some white on them, showed up against dark floors and were much easier to see than dark clothing. She made it to her seat without tripping or running into anybody, and breathed a sigh of relief as she settled in to watch the movie. When the feature ended she waited for the lights to come up and most of the crowd to disperse before she made her way slowly and carefully across the lobby and out onto the sidewalk, remembering to put her hand out in front of her to make sure she was walking through the door and not into a glass wall.

Her strategy for walking across what surely must have been several acres of parking area between the theatre and the motel, was to move between the pools of light cast by the street lights while watching for curbs, intermittent patches of ice, and the headlights of vehicles. It was a tedious, nerve-wracking journey and seemed to take forever, but it was still a piece of cake compared to how hard it had been to navigate the inside of the theatre. On the plus side, when she finally got back to her motel room, she was tired enough to go right to sleep.

Sitting on the plane the next day, she decided that while she was not sorry she'd gone to the theatre, she would probably not be attending any more movies by herself. There was a fine line between doing what she could do, and taking unnecessary risks. She didn't think that she'd crossed that line last night, but it had been close. Either theatres were getting darker, or her vision was getting worse.

• • •

Diana's aversion to grocery carts stemmed from the day she had inadvertently knocked over a cardboard kiosk displaying seasoning packets. The store clerk had been very nice as Diana apologized for the jumble of packets littering the floor. The good news was that they weren't breakable, but they would certainly have to be sorted out after they were picked up.

"I told our manager this display was too big to be in the aisle and it was going to get knocked over!" the clerk said, shaking her head. "He never listens to anyone around here!"

Diana wondered if the woman was telling the truth, or just trying to make a clumsy customer feel better. Since that incident, Diana used the hand-held shopping baskets which had the added benefit of holding about the same number of items that would easily fit into her backpack.

• • •

Diana had copies of her RP exam and diagnosis from Dr. Letz forwarded to her local eye doctor. Dr. Johns apologized for not picking up on her symptoms of RP, explaining that he had only seen two cases in his entire career. He referred her to an ophthalmologist in Great Falls, which was much closer than Seattle, so of course it was easier to get someone to give her a ride to and from her appointment. She might not have made the switch so easily, except that two years after Diana first met him, Dr. Letz had retired and sold his practice to Dr. Liza Rosen.

On her first visit to Dr. Rosen, Diana was told she needed to have laser surgery for glaucoma as soon as possible, and she was referred to a surgeon. Not about to quibble on an eye-related issue, Diana returned to Seattle by train later that same month -- as soon as the appointment for eye surgery could be scheduled. She checked into a motel and made arrangements for a town car to transport her to and from the surgeon's office the next day. Gray, her sons, and one of her cousins had offered to go with her, worried that she shouldn't be alone to have eye surgery, but Diana insisted that she didn't need anyone to babysit her for an outpatient procedure. She was so cranky about it that in spite of their misgivings, they all acquiesced to her wishes. After filling out new pa-tient and insurance paperwork, she waited in an exam room. Her eyes were dilated and she waited some more. Finally the surgeon examined her and sent her back to the waiting room. The eye surgeon was tall and broad-shouldered with wavy dark hair and he was very young. Or at least he seemed young to Diana. When her name was called again, she was escorted to his office. He gestured for her to be seated and then sat behind his desk.

"I'm not quite sure why you were sent to see me," he said, "because I double checked everything, and you do not need glaucoma surgery."

"Well, that's good news, isn't it?" Diana said, trying very hard to focus on the blessing of not needing laser surgery, instead of on the travel, the expense, the inconvenience and the stress she'd incurred be-cause of a misdiagnosis. She was really glad she had insisted that she was perfectly capable of handling this on her own; since it turned out that there was nothing to handle except getting back home.

Diana thought that perhaps if Dr. Rosen had possessed a bit more experience, she might have re-checked her test numbers, especially in light of the fact that Diana had not previously shown any signs of glaucoma. Surely that information was in her chart? Diana also knew some of the blame was her own because she should have asked a few more questions or asked for the test to be double-checked. Well, lesson learned. She would pay more attention and ask more questions.

She assumed that Dr. Rosen would learn the importance of double-checking as she traveled the path from young and educated to mature and experienced. Diana liked her and might have continued to see her had it not been for the travel required to be her patient. Instead, she decided to give Dr. Thomas a try.

• • •

Diana saw Dr. Thomas every three months, and her eye appointments with always started the same way. First she saw one or more of the assistants for the vision tests, and then she waited in an examination room for Dr. Thomas. On her first visit, she did warn them about that peripheral vision exam, but of course they had to find out for themselves. They never bothered to run that test again.

Dr. Thomas was tall and slender, with white hair and a brisk, no-nonsense manner. After he reviewed her chart, he checked her eye pressures and looked into her eyes with bright lights. Knowing it was necessary, she still dreaded that part of the exam because it always gave her a headache and left her nauseous for an hour or two afterwards.

"Hmm." Dr. Thomas said, looking at her chart. This too, was something that happened every time. He looked at her chart, apparently reading whatever his assistants had written and said, 'hmmm'. Diana decided to have some fun with him.

"Would that be a good 'hmmm' or a bad 'hmmm?'" she asked, smiling.

"Oh, a good one, certainly." Dr. Thomas answered, looking up with a smile of his own. "There has been no appreciable change in your vision since your last visit."

"Is that unusual?" Diana asked, curiously.

"A little, yes. Most RP patients show a more rapid decline." Dr. Thomas explained. "But we always appreciate good news." He set her file down and reached for the light switch to darken the room for her exam.

"I got my driver's license renewed last week." Diana said, casually. Dr. Thomas whipped around so fast she thought he might have given himself whiplash.

"But you don't drive, do you?" he asked sharply.

"Oh no, I walk everywhere I need to go, I just wanted to see if I could pass the eye test." Diana assured him. "And it is handy to have a driver's license as a picture I.D."

"You can get a picture I.D. instead, you know." Dr. Thomas explained.

"I'll probably do that next time." She assured him. "I think it is a little scary that according to the State of Montana, I see well enough to drive, though, don't you?"

"Yes, I do. Be very careful, even walking around." Dr. Thomas cautioned, and Diana assured him that she was.

• • •

Walking around town doing her errands one day, Diana was taking a short cut that involved crossing an alley behind Gray's office. She saw a pickup coming and waited for it to pass. When it had gone by and she was just about to step out, she heard the clang of metal and looked down, startled to see that the pickup was towing an empty flat-bed trailer like the kind she had seen loaded with snowmobiles or motorcycles or lawn mowing equipment. With her heart pounding, she waited for the trailer to move past her. She reminded herself that this was one of the dangers of not having peripheral vision; she had not noticed the trailer, had not seen it at all. The kindergarten jingle she'd learned so many years ago popped into to her mind.

"Stop, look and listen, before you cross the street. Use your eyes, use your ears, and then use your feet."

They were words to live by, and her ears had just saved her from a nasty accident. The danger in navigating around town encompassed more than dodging low-hanging tree branches, and watching for cracks in the sidewalk.

• • •

The inside of any store always seemed dim, especially in comparison to the sunshine outside. The floor of the grocery store in Shelby was covered in industrial linoleum and it was a light gray color. That made it easier for Diana to navigate, even though she still had to move carefully to avoid running into other shoppers, their carts, or employees. She had nearly fallen over a man kneeling on the floor as he re-stocked the bottom shelf one day, and several times had just about taken a header over pallets of supplies waiting to be shelved.

Keeping her eyes lowered to the floor to compensate for her lack of peripheral vision meant that sometimes other shoppers thought she was ignoring them, and although she was sorry to give off that vibe, there wasn't anything she could do about it, short of wearing a sign around her neck or a tee-shirt that read, "I'm not stuck up, I just don't see you".

When other shoppers spoke to her, she was more than happy to stop and chat, and if she didn't always know to whom she was speaking, she kept that information to herself. Sometimes she could figure out who she was talking to from their voice, or from the conversation itself. Sometimes she couldn't and she went home still wondering who she had visited with.

• • •

Diana and Gray learned by trial and error what strategy worked best in a restaurant. Gray took Diana's hand or she took his arm when they entered, and he let her know if there were steps up or down and how many. She never sat facing a window because of the glare, usually kept her left hand on her beverage glass to avoid spilling whatever she was drinking, and if the light was too dim, needed the menu read to her. Usually by the time the food arrived, her eyes had adjusted so that she was able to make out at least the outline of her salad or entrée. She knew parts of their conversations would definitely sound odd if they were overheard.

"Is there any more chicken?" Diana asked. Gray glanced at her plate which had contained a chicken fajita salad.

"Looks like you got all the chicken. You missed a slice of avocado though, on your left." He answered.

• • •

It was a good thing that Diana enjoyed a variety of entrées that didn't need to be cut with a knife; halibut, salmon, and pasta, for example, because although he didn't mind, she hated to ask Gray to cut her meat for her. She listened carefully to the special, because it if sounded good, she didn't even need to worry about reading the menu. She ordered steak or prime rib sometimes, but only if she could see well enough to use a steak knife. Some dining rooms were darker than others, and some of them turned the lights lower as the evening grew later. Diana learned this by accident when she and Gray were out for dinner and she noticed there was enough light for her to see pretty well. She ordered prime rib, and just as the plate was set in front of her, the lights in the dining room dimmed.

"Oh," Diana exclaimed jokingly to the server. "Who turned out the lights?"

"We dim them at 7:30." The server explained as she lit the candle in the middle of the table. "Is there anything else you need?" Diana thanked her and wished she'd ordered the halibut. Luckily the prime rib was very tender and she was able to cut most of it with a fork.

• • •

The weekend after her quarterly eye exam in Great Falls with Dr. Thomas, Diana and Gray exited their favorite Mexican restaurant and walked to the pickup. After they'd climbed in and closed their doors, Gray turned around.

"Just out of curiosity, did you mean to get into the back seat?" He asked. Diana looked around. Sure enough, she was sitting in the back seat of their crew cab.

"No!" She said, irritably. By the time she'd climbed out of the back seat and into the passenger seat, her sense of humor had re-asserted itself and she was laughing.

"I'm sure glad my eyes haven't gotten any worse, aren't you?"

• • •

One evening, in a particularly dark restaurant, one of their dining companions commented that it was so dark she didn't know what the vegetables were until she took a bite.

"Welcome to my world!" Diana joked.

• • •

"I thought you were going to wash that window yesterday." Gray commented as he sipped his morning coffee. Diana turned to look over her shoulder at the window above the kitchen sink. As a matter of fact, she had washed that window yesterday – inside and out – and after going over it several times, she had been confident that the glass would sparkle. Now, in the light of the morning sun, she realized that all she'd done was create streaks and smears. Without comment, she turned back around and focused on the crossword puzzle from the morning paper. Wisely, Gray didn't say any more either.

• • •

"So how are your eyes?" Jamie asked.

"Dr. Thomas says there has been no appreciable change, so I thought I was doing fine."

"But?"

"Gray decided that we need a cleaning lady."

"Good for him! I love having a cleaning lady, and I bet you will too!" Jamie exclaimed.

"Yeah, but you have a full-time job. I don't." It wasn't that Diana had ever pretended to like cleaning. On the contrary, she thought of housework as a necessary evil. For years she had joked that dust was a protective coating for the furniture, insisted her house was clean enough to be healthy and cluttered enough to be comfortable, and proclaimed that only neurotic women had immaculate homes. Still, she thought she was completely capable of cleaning her own house. She tried to explain that to Jamie.

"I just feel like I should do what I can do as long as I can do it."

"Apparently Gray thinks you can't do it anymore." Jamie said, bluntly.

"I guess so." Diana sighed. "I hate that I spill things, drop things, and break things so often. And Gray thinks it is easier if he just does things for me, so he won't have to clean up the mess I'd make if I did things myself."

"He should get points for trying to help, don't you think?"

"Probably." Diana grumbled."But it makes me feel useless and incompetent."

"How often is your cleaning lady going to come?"

"Twice a month." Diana replied.

"That's perfect! " Jamie said encouragingly. "You'll adjust really fast. Plus you'll still have all the daily stuff to do, and the laundry and the yard work. It isn't like you'll be sitting around twiddling your thumbs."

"I know, but there are a lot of things Gray doesn't want me to do anymore and it bugs me that I can't tell which ones I can handle and which ones I can't."

"Like what?"

"Gray fixes himself a smoothie for breakfast during the week, but on Sunday, we usually have eggs. I've cooked hundreds of eggs in my day. One would think I could cook eggs in my sleep, but several weeks ago, I over-salted them, and since then he sort of hovers and offers to do the salt and pepper. I can't blame him! Then last weekend I set the heat too high and the eggs got a little crispy on the bottom!"

"What did Gray say about that?"

"He just looked at me and shook his head. I bet he'll offer to cook the eggs next time."

"It won't kill him to cook his own eggs." Jamie assured her.

"I've been cooking since I was eight years old and all of a sudden I screw up the simplest things." Diana groaned. "It's annoying!"

• • •

The next time Diana and Jamie visited on the phone, Diana had another lament.

"I wanted to paint the guest room and Gray said we should hire someone. I mean, seriously? I spent one entire summer painting while I was in college. In our other house, I painted every room at least once while we lived there. I know how to paint!"

"If Gray thinks you can't see well enough to clean, I can understand why he wouldn't want you painting, though." Jamie suggested.

"Yeah, well, it was kind of a stupid thing to fight over I guess. I thought I could do it and he thought I couldn't. I finally decided if I was going to pay someone, I'd rather pay someone I knew, so I asked my new cleaning lady if she would be interested in helping me – not doing it for me. Jen agreed and we got everything taped and ready to go. She was going to do the edges with a brush and I was going to use the roller on the walls."

"How did that work out?" Jamie asked.

"I thought everything was going really well, and then Jen looked at the first wall I painted and suggested that I go paint in the closet. Apparently I missed whole strips of the wall. Then on the way to do the closet, I stepped in the paint tray!"

"It was a good thing Jen was helping you then, right?" Jamie said when she stopped laughing. "I hope you had a drop cloth on the carpet!"

● ● ●

"What happened here?" Gray asked nudging the envelope on the table with his forefinger.

"I think it's pretty obvious." Diana replied without looking up from the crossword puzzle. *Returned for Postage* was stamped on the front of the envelope in red ink.

"You forgot to put a stamp on it?" Diana did not answer. Earlier in the week, she had balanced her checkbook, which took awhile because she had entered two amounts into her register incorrectly. She wasn't sure if that was because of her eyesight, dyslexia, or carelessness. Then she had written checks, matched them with payment coupons, sealed them into envelopes and walked to the post office to put them in the mail. She remembered going through the stack of bills three times to make sure they all had return address stickers and stamps on them and in the correct places. She had been known to put the stamp on the back of the envelope and the address sticker on the bottom if she wasn't careful. When she arrived at the post office, she dropped the envelopes through the slot one at a time, checking them again. And still she managed to mail one without a stamp. Unbelievable! And she didn't want to hear about it, she just wanted the envelope, now with a stamp in the corner, mailed.

• • •

Mark had just brought her a bouquet of flowers for Valentine's Day. They were gorgeous and while Diana admired them and read the card, Mark tore a couple of paper towels off the roll, dampened them at the sink and went back to the entry where he scrubbed at the wall.

"What are you doing?" Diana asked curiously.

"When I came in I noticed a couple of smudges on the wall. I'm not sure what they are. They kinda look like blood." He stepped back and surveyed the wall. Apparently satisfied that he'd removed the spots, he grinned at his mother and said, "I sure hope I didn't just clean up a crime scene."

Diana had to laugh, and she also had to admit that Mark got his sense of humor from her. She thought the spots on the wall might have been chocolate fingerprints from her grandchildren. If Mark hadn't spotted them, Jen would have noticed when she came the next day to clean, or Gray would have seen them. No biggie.

• • •

Gray and Diana were on their way back to Shelby from Bozeman and had stopped for gas at a convenience store in Helena. Gray was filling the tank while Diana went into the store to use the restroom and then to purchased drinks and snacks. There was something about riding in a motorized vehicle that gave her the munchies, and munchies had to be washed down with a drink, which led to the need for a restroom. Funny how that worked, Diana thought. It felt good to get out of the pickup and walk around a little.

The inside of the store was dim, but the floor was light colored, so she found the restroom and made her purchases before she walked back outside to the gas pumps where their black pickup was parked. She opened the door, and if it hadn't been for the brightly colored seat covers, she would have climbed right in. Gray's pickup didn't have seat covers, brightly colored or otherwise, and she realized immediately that this was the wrong pickup. She closed the door and looked around, spotting another black pickup at the next pump. This time she checked the license plate before she opened the door so she knew it was the right one.

Diana didn't mention her latest blunder to Gray. It had happened because she assumed that she knew where the pickup was parked instead of looking carefully, including glancing at the license plate as she usually did. Years of experience had proved to her that assuming she knew what she was looking at was a bad idea, and yet, periodically, she did it anyway.

● ● ●

When she was still driving, Diana always opted for the drive-up window of the bank. When she quit driving, she began using the walk-up window. Sometimes it was necessary to go inside the main bank building, but it was dimly lit, so she avoided it whenever possible. On this day, she had to sign some papers for a loan she and Gray were re-doing in order to take advantage of lower interest rates. Gray took her arm on the way in, guiding her around the chairs and low tables that littered their path across the lobby to the president's office. They completed their business, chatted for a few minutes and stood to leave. Gray turned back to respond to a comment, and Diana, mistaking the glass wall for the doorway, ran into it. The two men spoke simultaneously.

"Are you okay?" asked the bank president.

"Sorry, I should have had your arm." Gray murmured. Diana laughed it off, as usual.

"My fault," she said cheerfully, and she was glad she had been edging out of the room instead of striding towards what she thought was the door of that office. She wondered why people used glass walls. They were hard to keep clean and provided no privacy.

CHAPTER 9

Old Friends

• • •

ONE DAY, DIANA NOTICED HER old high school classmate's name in the news. The two of them had lost touch as people do whose lives go off in different directions. She wrote Kay a letter and suggested they catch up. One thing led to another and before long, she was planning a weekend reunion with Kay and Lynn. They decided to meet in Missoula where Lynn was visiting family and Kay had a continuing education seminar. Diana arrived on the Greyhound bus.

"Wow, can you believe we are back together after forty years! My mind is pinging along so fast I don't even know what to say first." Lynn said, with a smile on her face and a twinkle in her eye. The three old friends were ensconced in a motel room, each holding a wine glass. A freshly opened bottle of champagne sat nestled in an ice bucket on the small table between the two matching easy chairs occupied by Lynn and Kay. Diana lounged against the pillows on the bed. Lynn, always organized, had provided both the champagne and the wine glasses.

"Then I'll start!" Kay said, as she picked up the bottle and filled each glass and then raised hers. "First, I propose a toast to Diana! For sending me that letter when she saw my name in the paper. It was a most welcome blast from the past!" Three wine glasses tinkled as they touched.

"We need to catch up before we do anything else. Okay?" Kay said. Diana and Lynn nodded and settled back to listen. "By the time you two were out of college, I had a three year old and we'd moved, and then I decided to get a job, so I ran for justice of the peace."

"Why?" Diana asked.

"Good pay, good benefits and flexible hours, mostly." Kay replied. "I didn't want to do a minimum wage job, and with just a high school diploma... Well anyway, you know me, I go overboard with everything, but in politics, that's good. I went door to door and talked to everyone who would listen, and I got elected. Then I had to go to judge school and learn about the law and pass a test to be able to actually have the job. It was the first time I ever cared about school. I really got into it, and every time my term was up, I ran again, and I just kept getting re-elected."

"Do you feel like you have made a difference?" Lynn asked.

"Some days I do, and some days I don't." Kay replied. "It's probably like any other job. Sometimes it gets depressing, but it's all about people. People and their life stories have always fascinated me."

"What's the most fun part of your job?" Diana asked.

"Weddings! Some of them have been off-beat, and some of them have been downright weird – well, obviously people who are having a JP do their ceremony are not exactly traditional." Kay chuckled. "My husband always goes with me when I do weddings, because you never know what you'll run into. They are always interesting!"

"What's the worst thing about your job?" Lynn asked.

"I hate seeing kids in trouble. And I had a crazy guy stalk me for a couple of years and that was really scary." Kay replied with a shudder. "My husband is a Vietnam Vet, you know, and he has a license to carry a concealed weapon. He took me to and from work and sat in my courtroom, which made me feel a lot safer. Then I decided to go through the process to be able to carry a weapon."

"Seriously?" Diana asked. "You carry a gun? Where?"

"Seriously! In my purse. You do things you never expected to do when your life is threatened." Kay said. "It changes how you look at things. You learn to stay alert and take precautions. But you also learn to enjoy the little things to try to keep things in perspective and alleviate the stress."

"Shall we have a toast to the unexpected twists and turns of life?" Diana asked. Her two friends nodded and the three of them raised their glasses.

"You next, Lynn." Kay urged.

"Okay. Well, like you, I have a tendency to go a little bit overboard." Lynn began. Her two friends snickered but she ignored them and went on. "I got married after my sophomore year in college, graduated and then had kids while I was finishing up my Masters."

"Does that surprise you?" Diana directed her question at Kay. "That she did it all at once?"

"Nope." Kay replied. Lynn continued as if they hadn't spoken.

"We moved several times, and each time I got a different job." She listed some of the jobs she'd had while they moved around the country. She'd been, among other things, a county extension agent, a counselor, an office manager and a salesperson.

"What kind of sales?" Kay asked curiously. "I can't picture you working in retail."

"Uh, no. I sold cemetery plots." Lynn replied. Stunned silence greeted this announcement.

"Why on earth would you do that?" Kay asked when she finally found her tongue.

"Why not? The hours were flexible and the pay was good. Similar reasons to the ones you had when you got into being a JP, right?"

"Okay…" Kay agreed, uncertainly. "So what happened then?"

"Well, some of the people I'd sold plots to started needing them. That wasn't so much fun." Lynn said. "And then we moved again and my next job was doing home mortgages."

"Okay – same questions – tell us the best and worst parts of your jobs." Diana prompted.

"That would take all night!" Lynn protested. "I've had too many jobs and they were too different. I'm going to say the best part of my life was moving – I've always loved moving to new places, meeting new people, and trying new things. And the worst part of my life was right before we moved – when I got bored and restless." There was a moment of silence before Kay shook her head and raised her glass and then Diana raised hers too. With a grin, Lynn touched her glass to theirs and, with no need for words they sipped in a silent toast. Then Kay turned to Diana.

"I'll be brief, because I'm happy with my life, but it isn't very exciting. I got married after graduation and we moved a couple of times before we ended up in Shelby. Unlike either of you, I was a full-time stay-at-home mother without a quote, unquote, real job. All of our kids live close enough that we see them and our grandchildren often."

"Sounds like a pretty nice life to me!" Kay said.

"I agree! " Lynn chimed in.

"Okay, now that we're caught up, I think we should share what we are focusing on now. We're all going to be sixty this year. That's a new decade as well as a huge milestone." Kay picked up the role of moderator again. "In my job I see a lot of pain and tragedy and hopelessness, so I'm trying to identify the things that bring me joy. First on the list is spending time with my family and friends, of course. And I have been taking classes in painting and sculpting and different things like that because focusing on creating beauty feeds my soul."

"Very profound!" Lynn said. "Diana? You can be next."

"I guess you could say that I'm retired, and from my perspective, it isn't all it's cracked up to be." Diana said ruefully.

"Are you talking about empty nest?" Lynn asked.

"More like empty life, I think. First I was a kid with too much responsibility, then I worked my way through college, and after that I got married and had a family. If there is a downside to being a full-time mother, it's that I sort of lost me, or maybe I never knew who I was to begin with." Diana made a face and went on. "With the kids grown up and gone, I definitely have empty nest. But I don't have anything else I am passionate about, so I guess my main goal right now is trying to figure me out. Isn't that classic – I'm a child of the sixties trying to find myself – at sixty!"

"I think most people our age are at some kind of a crossroads in life, thinking about or adjusting to retirement, dealing with empty nest, coping with health issues or with the death of a spouse, caring for aging parents, or going through a divorce like I am." Lynn commented. Her two friends looked at her in surprise.

"Explain! What's this about a divorce?" Kay demanded.

"We were never compatible, and I finally decided I couldn't live like that anymore. So I'm focusing on spiritual growth as part of the process of dissolving my marriage and turning my life in a new direction. It is both scary and exciting and to be honest -- I thought I was unique, but I've learned that divorce at this time of life isn't all that uncommon."

"Of course you are unique – all of us are. But I had no idea you weren't happily married." Kay replied. "I'm sorry to hear that. When we got married, nobody expected it to last, so we really had to depend on each other. We sort of grew up together, and we are still best friends. We've been lucky, I guess."

"Yes, you have." Lynn agreed.

" Diana, how is your marriage?" Kay asked.

"Well, that was subtle!" Diana replied, rolling her eyes. "We fight a lot."

"Where there's sparks there's fire?" Kay asked with a smirk.

"Not going there!" Diana replied, shaking her head.

"So what do you fight about?" Lynn wanted to know. "The big three are money, sex and in-laws." Diana thought about that, briefly, then shook her head.

"I think we disagree because we are oldest children and both of us want to run things."

"Let's drink to fighting and having great make-up sex!" Lynn suggested, laughing.

"Who brought sex into this conversation?" Diana demanded.

"I did!" Lynn said, still laughing, "I'm not getting any, but I'm assuming you two are. I should at least get to talk about it."

"Moving on here, girls!" Kay interrupted. "Since we have discussed our past and our present, next we need to discuss what you see in your future. Diana?"

"While I'm trying to find myself, I've been keeping busy with gardening, reading, and brushing up on my piano, but I don't really have a goal. The thing is, I've always had a goal; to graduate from high school, to figure out a way to pay for college, to be a good mother, or to help my husband build a business. Plus, I never really expected to live this long, so I didn't plan on getting old – and now I feel like I don't have a goal. I'm making it up as I go along, and it is driving me crazy."

"Hey!" Lynn objected. "What's wrong with making it up as you go along? I've been doing that forever and I kinda like it! Course I never planned on getting old either, come to think of it."

"Oh please! Nobody plans on getting old. But there's a difference between not planning on getting old and not planning to live very long. I think Diana meant that she thought she'd die young, right Diana?" Kay asked.

"Well, my mom died young, so I realized that it was a possibility, at least." Diana answered with a shrug.

"So, maybe that's why you've always been so cautious." Lynn commented. "Kay, your dad died young. Did you ever think you might die young too?"

"I knew it was a possibility, so I decided to live large, just in case." Kay replied, candidly.

"Well, that explains a lot about the two of you and your approach to life." Lynn said thoughtfully. "Kay wanted to do as much as possible in case she ran out of time, and Diana tried not to take too many chances."

"When you put it like that, I want to be Kay!" Diana protested.

"Honestly!" Kay rolled her eyes. "Neither one of us died young, so that's that. Moving on; I am not buying your idea you don't have a plan, Lynn. You always have a plan!"

"Nope, no plan." Lynn said. "Your turn."

"Huh. Well, I've got to work a few more years before I can afford it, but I am starting to think about retirement. I've got at least a bazillion hobbies so I think I'll enjoy it."

"A bazillion hobbies, huh?" Diana asked curiously. "Like what?"

"I collect mannequins and dress them up for holidays and parties. I make and market my own soaps and lotions; sometimes I give soap-making classes. I make jewelry, and recently got interested in dolls. We have a big garden and we go camping and fishing with our son and his family, and our dogs."

"It amazes me that you went into the judicial system when your temperament is so artistic." Lynn commented.

"Possibly she has a previously undetected split-personality, and needs counseling!" Diana laughed. "Lynn! Put on your counseling hat!" Kay rolled her eyes.

"Possibly I just have a well balanced personality, did you ever consider that? Anyway, we are discussing, not analyzing!" Kay stated. "And I'm not done with what I see for my future! I've got a really good relationship with my grandson. He's going to be heading to college in a couple of years. Realistically, I could be looking at becoming a great grandmother before I'm seventy. I think that might be kinda cool, to be honest."

"Do you?" Diana asked curiously. "I'm just getting the hang of being a grandmother. I can't imagine being a 'great'!"

"I think you'd be 'great' at it, Kay. Pun intended." Lynn asserted. "I can totally see you as a great-grandmother!"

"We do stay true to form, don't we?" Kay laughed. "Diana is cautious and Lynn is gung-ho. But let's get back to the question. Lynn, you are next. What do you see in your future?"

"Well, dissolving my marriage cut my net worth in half, and that's only fair so I'm not complaining, but I need to build my financial reserves back up before I can afford to retire, so for the next few years, I see myself continuing to work and travel and meet new people. What I would really like to do is establish a retirement career. I want to be a writer and be good enough to make some money at it."

"Did I not just say a few short minutes ago, that you always have a plan?" Kay asked. "I rest my case."

"It's more a dream than a plan at this stage." Lynn argued. Kay, Lynn and Diana talked late into the night, and then early into the morning, picking up the threads of their relationship as if they'd never been apart. Their conversation swirled and bounced from opinion to philosophy, from memories of the past to plans for the future.

The next day, as they were in Lynn's car on their way to the mall for some shopping, Diana finally broached the subject of her deteriorating eyesight. Briefly she explained what RP was, and listed the symptoms.

"And you are just now telling us this because?" Kay said indignantly. Lynn was giving Diana a dirty look too.

"I didn't mention it yesterday because I was enjoying catching up, I guess. Plus I really hate to make everything about me all the time. Everyone is dealing with something, especially at our age, right? It could be worse. But I'll probably need help at the mall, so…"

"So what kind of help do you need when we go into the mall?" Lynn asked.

"Depends on how dim the lighting is and how dark the floor is. Sometimes I do okay, and other times I might need an arm." They spent the day mostly window-shopping, making occasional purchases if something caught their eye.

"What color is this?" Diana asked, holding up a long-sleeved knit pullover in a flowered print.

"Navy." Lynn replied. "What color did you think it was?"

"Either navy or black, I have trouble telling the difference."

"How do you know what color pants you are wearing then?" Kay asked curiously.

"When I buy a new pair, I mark the label with a 'B' or an 'N' with one of those laundry pens, and I use a 'G' for charcoal gray." Diana replied. "I do the same with shirts, if I can't tell."

• • •

Six months later Diana and her two high school friends again spent a weekend together.

"It's a fine balance between trying to be helpful and just plain getting in her way, isn't it?" Lynn asked with a laugh as Diana looked ruefully down at her wet feet and shrugged. She had just walked through a puddle.

"That's for sure!" Lynn agreed. "I grabbed her arm to go across the street and she had no trouble with the curb, then I thought she was fine, so I didn't have ahold of her and she walked right through that puddle!"

"And ten minutes ago, we warned her about the garbage can, and then she bumped into that hanging planter." Lynn shook her head.

"Hey!" Diana defended herself. "She would gladly explain to you how to help her, but as you may have noticed, she has absolutely no idea what she can't see!" All three of them laughed.

Diana had not expected Lynn and Kay to figure things out during an occasional weekend. It had taken several months for her to learn to coach Gray so he could help her. She remembered telling him that he needed to give her specific directions like to go straight ahead, take three steps, or turn right, because pointing, telling her to 'watch out', or saying 'over there', wasn't helpful.

CHAPTER 10

Technology

• • •

DIANA HAD BEEN A LOVER of books since first grade when she learned to read. She got her first library card that year, and checked out several books per week throughout her childhood. Her mom read to her and her siblings at bedtime, but Diana did not see her reading for her own enjoyment. Like many a homemaker in the fifties, she grew a garden, cooked and baked from scratch, and sewed her own clothes and clothes for her children. In contrast, Diana's dad, though he worked hard and had many hobbies, was always in the middle of a book, and Diana shared his passion for a good read.

As a young woman she checked books out of the library, bought paperbacks, borrowed books from friends, and subscribed to numerous magazines. As she got older, reading began to give her headaches, and the smaller print used in magazines and the daily newspaper became harder for her to decipher. Well, she reasoned, that was part of getting older. She got stronger glasses, and that helped some, but it wasn't enough, so she bought a full-page magnifier with a light. It was a little inconvenient to use, but she had fewer headaches, so it was worth it.

Then Cole and his wife gave her a Kindle for Christmas. Beth was a fellow book lover. She used her kindle mostly when she traveled and thought it would make reading easier for Diana because she could easily increase the text size. There was a definite learning curve, but once Diana figured out how to use it, she quickly became addicted to it.

• • •

"What do you like best about your Kindle?" Lynn asked as they sat on the deck enjoying the sunset.

"Lots of things." Diana replied. "Being able to adjust the text size, of course, and not having to store the books I buy. I also like being able to have all my books in my purse, especially when I travel."

"Do you re-read books?" Lynn asked.

"Not as much as I used to." Diana laughed. "More often than I'd like to admit, I would buy a paperback and realize after I started it that I'd read it before. When I buy books from Amazon, they very helpfully tell me if I've already purchased that book. I love that feature!"

"Me too!" Lynn agreed.

"I figure as my memory goes, I'll be able to re-read all the books on my kindle as if they were brand new!" Diana quipped and both women chuckled.

• • •

Mark and Sue gave Diana a cell phone for Christmas. Mark showed her how to use it and asked her to always carry it with her. It didn't take long for her to get used to having a phone in her pocket or her purse. Within a year after she got her phone, she added texting to her plan.

"You text? That surprises me." Jamie said as she joined Diana at the table. Things were winding down at the wedding reception for her oldest son, and she had noticed Diana reading and responding to a text message on her phone.

"It surprises me too," Diana admitted. "But my kids are on the road all the time, lots of times driving in bad weather. For some reason, they just won't pick up the phone and call to let me know that they arrived safely, but they will text 'home'. Go figure."

"Do you text a lot then?" Jamie wanted to know.

"I thought I would text mostly with my kids. That was Riley wanting to know how the wedding was and if we were having a good time. But I seem to be doing more of it, so when I upgraded my phone last year, I got one with a keyboard." Diana replied, and then couldn't resist sharing the story of her first phone upgrade with Jamie.

• • •

Diana had gone into the Verizon store, happy to see they weren't very busy. Approaching the counter, she pulled her phone out and laid it on the glass counter.

"I need to get a new phone." She told the young woman behind the counter. "The buttons on this one are starting to stick."

"My goodness!" The young woman exclaimed. "How long have you had this phone?"

"I don't know - four or five years, I guess, why?" Diana replied. The woman held it up to show the other sales person in the store, a young man whom Diana judged to be in his early twenties.

"Look at this!" she exclaimed. He came over to examine the phone and proclaimed with mock seriousness, that it must be an antique. Diana rolled her eyes at the two of them and they all laughed as they began the process of upgrading her phone. She decided that they might have been right about it being an antique when they had trouble finding a cable to fit so they could transfer her information to the new one. Eventually, she left with a new phone and embarked on another learning curve.

In theory, Diana believed in stepping outside of her comfort zone and trying new things. She didn't want to be one of those elderly people who refused to listen to new ideas because she had known people like that and they annoyed her. That was in theory. The reality was a little more complicated, but she made an honest attempt to keep an open mind about everything, especially technological things. By the time she needed another upgrade, phones had evolved to the point where she asked Sue to go with her and help her choose options.

• • •

One of the fun things her sons did was to text her pictures of her grand-kids. Cole noticed a color picture taped to his mother's refrigerator of his daughter Leah, age three, in a three point football stance in their backyard.

"Is this the picture I texted you?" he asked.

"Yeah." Diana said, "It was so cute I wanted a hard copy."

"How did you do that?" Cole asked, looking at her in astonishment.

"Oh, I e-mailed it to myself, and then used the color printer to print it out." Diana said. "I wasn't sure if that would work, but it did."

"Wow! Go Mom!" Cole laughed, and she gave him a mock bow.

• • •

Diana's generation grew up before televisions were a common house-hold item. Stations started broadcasting in the afternoon with cartoons and children's programming. The six o'clock news was followed by family programming and the station went off the air after the late eve-ning news. In college, computers were so bulky that they took up an entire building. When Gray opened his first office, the computer he bought was about the size of a desk. He kept up with technology and made the switch to personal desk top computers as soon as they became available. Diana got her first desktop when Mark was in middle school and subscribed to dial-up internet when it became available in their area several years after that -- about the time Mark went off to college.

Gray insisted his office computers be updated every three years, and Diana's computer at home was part of that mandate. She accepted those upgrades with as much grace as she could muster. It seemed to her that there was always a glitch of some kind to work through, and after every upgrade, there was a new learning curve, which once she adjusted to, she didn't mind, but the adjustment period was challenging. In other words, Diana appreciated technology, but using it did not come naturally to her.

Sometimes she thought that she had somehow been skipped when they were passing out the technology gene. Both her sisters seemed to have it. Her sister Joy had majored in business education, then became a computer programmer. Gray and Diana had given Marcy a re-furbished computer after one of their office upgrades. Marcy had purchased a how-to book, read it cover to cover, and before Diana realized what had happened, Marcy was doing all kinds of things with her computer that Marcy had never heard of, much less attempted. It was more than a little intimidating.

• • •

"You should get an Ipad." Jamie's e-mail informed her. "They are so much fun, but besides that, I think you'd find it convenient and really easy to use. They have adjustable text size like your kindle, plus you can enlarge whatever is on the screen if you need to. They take great pictures, and you can play games and read books on them. You said having your kindle was like carrying a library in your purse – well having an Ipad would be like having a computer in your purse, but without the mouse. You mentioned that you have trouble finding the curser – the Ipad uses a touch screen. Super easy! Think about it!"

By this time, Diana had graduated from a desktop computer to a laptop, which she hooked up to a big screen for her work at home. She wanted to take her computer with her when she traveled, so she chose the model with a white case and keyboard instead of a black one, and got the larger model with a bigger screen. She did take it with her when she traveled, and it was better than not having a computer, but was somewhat bulky and not exactly lightweight.

So at Jamie's suggestion, she thought about getting an Ipad. She thought about it for a couple of weeks while she did some research of her own and talked to people who had them. She considered Jamie's advice in context – her husband and all her children were technology junkies who lived, breathed, and worked with computers. In the end though, she bought an Ipad, almost entirely because she trusted Jamie's analysis and opinion.

• • •

Diana had to get someone who possessed the technology gene to help set up her new Ipad, but once that was done; she couldn't believe she had ever lived without it. She used it to check her e-mail away from home, added Facebook to her communications repertoire as a way to keep in touch with family and friends, had several Words with Friends games going at any given time, and played Sudoku and FreeCell.

She had read somewhere that logic games and crossword puzzles helped keep the brain active, and she was determined to do everything she could to help maintain her cerebral function. The knowledge that her dad had been in a nursing home with dementia by the age of sixty-nine did not lurk in her subconscious. It crept to the front of her mind and waved a big red flag at every opportunity, accompanied by loud warning bells and sirens. And Diana paid attention. Her morning regime included doing puzzles in the newspaper while she drank her coffee. As she solved the Crypto-quote, the Sudoku and two crossword puzzles, she wondered when the print would be too small for her to decipher. She was pretty sure it would happen one day because reading the rest of the paper gave her a headache. But so far, she was still able to do the puzzles without too many problems.

Diana had given up taking pictures decades earlier when looking through the viewfinder of a 35 millimeter camera became too difficult. She had tried using a digital camera, without much success, and was one of the few parents who did not view ball games and school programs through the lens of a video camera. The Ipad, though, was a point and click phenomenon, and pictures could be deleted, edited, organized into albums, stored in the cloud, and e-mailed with a touch on the screen. At least they could once she figured out the procedures. She couldn't see the screen in bright sunlight, but for indoor pictures, on cloudy days or at night, it was great.

She had also gradually stopped listening to music on CD, not because she didn't enjoy music, but because she had trouble operating the stereo. She could still do it, but she had to use a flashlight and a magnifying glass to decipher the dials and buttons. Downloading music and organizing playlists on the Ipad, though, was, as Jamie had promised, "Super Easy."

• • •

Throughout her life, when other people whined about their health or complained about the circumstances in their lives, Diana's first inclination was to tell them to just adjust already. She didn't do it, of course, but she thought about it! Since finding out that she had RP, she had been trying to take her own advice, and it was an ongoing struggle. The simplest things took on complications she never would have expected.

Take her purse, for example. In her college days she had a macramé shoulder bag. Constructed of knotted jute and lined with a bright print, the bag was just the right size to carry money and minimal make-up, and was a neutral color that went with everything casual. It was trendy and practical and she used it until it fell apart. Then she went through a denim phase, which was understandable since her signature outfit was blue jeans, tee shirt and tennis shoes. When the kids were small she needed more of a tote bag than a purse, because they were forever asking her to hold something for them. At some point along the way, shopping for a new purse became a very frustrating experience. They were either too big or too small, but the biggest problem was that most of them had dark interiors.

She found it at Target – a leather purse in a light color and big enough for the usual things she kept in her purse; checkbook, cash, credit cards, pocket calendar, sunglasses, Tylenol and gum. The inside was also light colored, so it would be easy to see things in there, and it had a minimum of pockets. In theory, pockets and compartments seemed like a great idea, with a place for everything and everything in its place. However, in reality Diana could never remember which pocket or compartment she had put something in, and had finally come to the conclusion that having everything in one place worked best for her. It came with a matching make-up bag big enough to hold her mascara, lipstick and fingernail clipper, in addition to a few coins. And the clincher was that the bag was roomy enough for her kindle and her ipad.

She really liked having her electronic devices handy, especially in the car. She wished she enjoyed looking out the window of the pickup at the scenery, but conditions had to be just right or it was stressful instead. Bright sunlight hurt her eyes, even with sunglasses. Driving through the forest where they went from sun to shade and back to sun again reminded her of the strobe lights they used at dances in her youth. Riding in the dark on the highway was a disorienting glare of headlights from behind them as well as from oncoming traffic. Knowing that her depth perception was off did not make it easier to sit calmly when it looked as if they were in imminent danger of a head-on collision. In town, the lights of businesses, some blinking or neon-colored, added to the visual chaos and gave her a headache. Yes, Gray was a good driver and she trusted him, but her reflexive reactions often slipped out as gasps and shudders. She didn't think that was fair to him, so Diana read or played games while he drove. Maybe it wasn't fair to him to disengage by focusing on an electronic device, either, but sometimes one has to choose the lesser of two evils.

CHAPTER 11
Travel

• • •

"KAY AND I ARE PLANNING a trip to New York to visit Lynn." Diana told Gray. He got that look on his face that meant he was not thrilled.

"Who is going to keep an eye on you?"

"I do not need someone to keep an eye on me, I'm not a child!" she said irritably.

"Remember your trip to Costa Rica?" Gray reminded her. She remembered it all right. She had landed in Denver, turned her phone on and found two text messages, one from Gray and one from Mark. Both of them informed her that she'd left her wallet in the Great Falls airport. Through a sequence of events that still left her somewhat in awe of the way people in small towns looked after each other, her wallet had been found by someone who knew her, handed off to someone from Shelby who was in Great Falls that day, and delivered to Gray's office later that same afternoon – well before she made it to her final destination. Diana much preferred to focus on those positive points, rather than the fact that she had lost her wallet in the first place.

"I admit I left my wallet, but all it had in it was my driver's license and less than fifty dollars." Diana protested. "I was smart enough to keep my passport and most of my money in my backpack, so it worked out okay. And the rest of the trip was fine." The rest of the trip had been fine because of Shelly, but that was another story. Diana would not have gone to Costa Rica in the first place if Shelly hadn't been there too. Shelly's husband was disabled and her years of experience in helping him, combined with her natural empathy made her a near perfect traveling companion. She was easy going, but observant, instinctively seeming to know whether to assist or stand back. Diana pulled her attention away from her memories of traveling with Shelly and back to her discussion with Gray.

"You'd probably fly through Minneapolis, and you aren't familiar with that airport." He objected. "Maybe you should request a wheelchair." Diana knew there had never been any doubt that she would go on this trip, because Gray had never been one to tell her what she could or could not do. But he would try to influence her plans.

She had, at the suggestion of a friend, requested a wheelchair on that Costa Rica trip, and readily admitted that it had been very convenient to be met at the plane and transported to her next flights in Denver and Dallas, and it was wonderful having someone to guide her through customs in Costa Rica. Even so, she had felt like a fraud since she was perfectly capable of walking.

"I'd rather not." She said. "I've been in the Minneapolis airport several times before and I didn't have any trouble. Plus I can always ask someone if I get lost." She hadn't told him, or anyone, really, about the time she had gotten lost in the Los Angeles airport. She had to go from one end of the airport to the other, and had stopped to ask directions several times. Oddly enough, some of the airport employees didn't seem to know anything about the airport other than the immediate area in which they worked. She supposed it was a similar situation to living in a large city where most people are familiar with their own neighborhood, but couldn't give directions off the top of their head to specific places across town. She had finally found signs that pointed the way to her next gate and everything was fine until she reached a place where the corridor she was in branched off in two directions, and neither of them had her gate listed. Perplexed, she stopped and turned in a full circle looking down each of the two new corridors and also back the way she had come, uncertain what to do. Just then, a man came striding towards her from the corridor on the left. He wore dark slacks and a white shirt, had an airport identification tag hanging around his neck, and was the only person she'd seen in the past few minutes. Clearly this wasn't a major thoroughfare.

She stopped him, held out her itinerary, and asked if he could help her find the gate she was looking for. He looked at her itinerary, looked at the signage, and checked her itinerary again, frowning. Then his expression cleared and he pointed behind her.

"You have to go up those stairs."

Diana turned, and even knowing where to look, it took her several moments to discern the stairway. She wasn't quite sure he knew what he was talking about, but she thanked him anyway, and started up the stairs. Sure enough, the sign for her gate was at the top of the stairway, and she found her gate without any more problems. She doubted anyone cared, but LAX had dropped to the bottom of her list of preferred airports, because in her opinion at least, it was not user friendly!

• • •

On the rare occasions when Diana flew alone, she always booked an aisle seat. She had just gotten settled when a young man approached and politely informed her that she must be in the wrong place because he had booked the aisle seat.

"We can ask the flight attendant if you wish, but I'm pretty sure I am in the right seat." Diana said pleasantly. The young man's shoulders slumped in defeat and he grumbled that he guessed it didn't really matter. Diana guessed it did matter, and an idea occurred to her.

"If having the aisle seat is important to you, maybe we could make a deal." Diana suggested. At the young man's raised eyebrows, she explained that she had bad eyes and couldn't tell when the flight attendant was handing her something, or speaking to her, for that matter. She said that if he would be willing to help her with those things, she would happily switch seats with him. He readily agreed and Diana moved to the window seat so he could sit on the aisle. True to his word, he courteously dealt with the handing out of refreshments and the picking up of garbage by the flight attendants. Diana thought he might be claustrophobic or possibly had ADHD because he had trouble sitting still, and she was glad she'd taken the window seat so he didn't have to get by her every time he left his seat.

• • •

Diana thought that if she was careful, moved at a leisurely pace, and asked for help as needed, she was completely capable of traveling unaccompanied. That was her opinion and she was sticking to it. Gray didn't agree, and he wasn't the only one. Kay, Lynn and Diana had quite a telephone discussion about whether or not Diana should travel alone.

"Fine!" Diana said, a lot less graciously than she would have liked. "I'll get someone to give me a ride to Billings and Kay and I can travel together from there so that she can babysit me."

"Perfect!" Lynn commented.

"I knew you'd see it my way." Kay said with a smirk in her voice. Diana didn't think her vision issues were a big deal. Everyone she knew had something they were dealing with, including her two friends. Lynn was developing arthritis and Kay had sleep apnea and admitted to mild claustrophobia.

• • •

Kay was a take charge kind of person, and she was vigilant where Diana's vision problems were concerned, so by the time they checked their bags, got their boarding passes and cleared security, Diana was heartily sick of being referred to as a visually impaired person. At the end of the day as they were getting ready to land at their destination, her sense of humor was strained to the breaking point and she had begun to mentally refer to herself as a 'very irritated person' whenever Kay called for assistance for 'the visually impaired person'. It was understandable that Kay would speak clearly in a louder voice than Diana was accustomed to. Kay's husband was losing his hearing. Unfortunately, knowing the why of it did not make it less irritating. Several times that day, Diana caught herself rolling her eyes behind Kay's back, which made her feel petty and ungrateful. She knew Kay was doing her best to help, and she was also well aware that it was difficult for other people to know when she needed help and when she was okay on her own; if truth be told, Diana herself had trouble with that one. She nearly always thought she could see just fine; right up until the moment she tripped or ran into something. So far, at least, though it could still happen, Kay had not shouted that there was a blind woman coming through. Diana chuckled to herself and gathered her patience as she picked up her belongings and prepared to exit the plane.

Kay glanced surreptitiously across the aisle as the plane touched down to check on Diana. At the same time, she continued to chat. She was a consummate people person, making friends wherever she went, and she had struck up a conversation with her seatmate while at the same time keeping an eye on Diana, who looked like she was doing okay, at least for now. Honestly, keeping track of an adult who thought she could see perfectly well when she couldn't, was more of a challenge than she ever dreamed it would be. Kay compared it to shopping in a high end department store with a two year old holding a dripping ice cream cone. The question was not if, but when, there would be a disaster of epic proportions.

They made their way off the plane and found the baggage claim area where Lynn was waiting. They exchanged hugs and small talk while they waited for the luggage to appear. Once they were in Lynn's car, Lynn asked how their flight was.

"It was fine." Diana replied.

"Did Kay keep you from going into the men's bathroom, then?" Lynn asked with a grin.

"Barely!" Kay exclaimed. "Did you know she does that?"

"Oh, yeah." Lynn chuckled. Diana rolled her eyes and turned to stare out the car window with a smile tugging at her mouth.

"Well," Lynn recalled with a laugh, "I was just coming in from getting gas, and there she was, too far away for me to stop her, heading straight into the men's room."

"What happened?" Kay demanded.

"Nothing happened!" Diana insisted. "The nice gentleman at the sink told me I was in the wrong bathroom, and I left."

"At least she thought he was at the sink." Lynn chuckled. "We'll never know for sure, he could have been standing at the urinal."

"Oh my God!" Kay groaned. "I managed to grab her arm, but she was headed for the wrong restroom at the airport too." She turned to Diana and asked. "Does that happen often?"

"I have a don't ask, don't tell policy on that." Diana replied, loftily. "And anyway, it's not a big deal. Lots of people go into the wrong restrooms!" At their skeptical looks, she told them about the time she saw a slightly inebriated man walk confidently into a women's bathroom at a restaurant only to exit a heartbeat later with a very red face. Catching her eye, he pointed a thumb over his own shoulder.

"There're no urinals in there!" he said incredulously.

"That might be because that's the ladies room." She told him, managing not to giggle. She kind of knew how he felt, after all. She also told Lynn and Kay about the time she'd followed a young woman into an airport restroom, which turned out to be the men's room. They rolled their eyes some more, so she decided not to tell them about her most embarrassing moment, at least so far. There could certainly be something worse in her future.

She and Gray were having dinner in an upscale restaurant. The restroom was dimly lit, with black granite counters, burgundy sinks, burgundy & silver striped wallpaper, dark colored tile, and cubicle walls that were either charcoal gray or black. She could hardly see inside the restroom, much less inside the cubicle, so she was relieved when she noticed the toilet paper trailing below the dispenser. At least she would not have to feel around on the wall to find the dispenser and then feel around some more to find the end of the tissue. She tore off a piece and was startled to hear a voice from the other side of the wall.

"Well, by all means, help yourself!" Apparently her toilet paper dispenser was on the other wall of the stall she was in!

• • •

On the first day of their visit, the three friends caught the ferry across the channel to Ellis Island. They took the audio tour looking at pictures and displays while they listened to tales of the immigrants who entered America through the golden door of Ellis Island. It was heartwrenching to hear about the rigors of the trip itself, and to contemplate the courage it took to leave everything familiar, with the clothes on your back and only the possessions you could carry, in order to pursue the hope of a better life in an unknown land. Their own ancestors had been among those immigrants, and they learned that the descendants of those twelve million immigrants account for almost half of the people in America today.

Their return trip was a bit of a challenge for all of them. The ferry was brightly lit, and the lights from the Statue of Liberty and the New York Skyline against the night sky were breathtakingly beautiful. But after the ferry docked at the pier, the magic dimmed considerably. Possibly because they were so busy chatting, they thought nothing of it when they parked, purchased their tickets and then walked through two enormous parking lots, down a street and out onto the pier. In the darkness, the distance seemed twice as far. There were streetlights spaced farther apart than they would have liked, and the now empty parking lot seemed eerie in the semi-darkness. Diana was the most cheerful and relaxed.

"Doesn't this bother you?" Kay asked irritably.

"Doesn't what bother me?"

"It's scary walking in the dark." Kay said, not exactly patiently.

"Welcome to my world!" Diana quipped. "It's dark and scary just about everywhere I go after dark, which is why I'm hanging on to your arm. You are responsible for keeping me safe. No pressure!"

• • •

The next two days were spent wandering through Time Square, mingling with the crowds of people and attending plays on Broadway. This was the highlight of Kay's trip. She loved both *Phantom of the Opera* and *Wicked.* When Kay was finally through taking pictures and buying souvenirs after the show, they worked their way through the crowd, making sure to keep a hand on Diana's arm so they didn't get separated. The idea of becoming separated worried Diana more than she cared to admit, so she paid close attention. Once free of the theatre crowd, they had to walk a couple of blocks before they could hail a cab. Kay got into the front seat while Diana and Lynn climbed into the back.

"The train station, please." Lynn said as the cab rolled forward.

"So, how long have you been driving a cab?" Kay asked. Before he could answer, Lynn spoke up from the back seat.

"Sir, it would save a lot of time and frustration if you'd just tell this nosy woman your entire life story right now and get it over with."

"Three years," the driver replied with a chuckle and a glance at Kay. She continued to pepper him with questions, including if he was a native of New York, if he was married, and did he have children. Earlier in the day, another cabbie had been much more talkative. He told Kay that his wife didn't work anymore because she had won the lottery.

"Are you serious?" Kay exclaimed.

"Oh yes – she married me!" The cabbie quipped with a grin. This cab driver was focused on his driving. He politely answered Kay's questions while the cab sat stuck in traffic, but his answers were brief and he kept his eyes on the street. Suddenly traffic started to move, and the cab sprang ahead with a jerk as he stepped on the gas. Kay rolled her window down and stuck her head out.

"Yee Haw!" she yelled at the top of her lungs. Lynn and Diana looked at each other in astonishment. Even the driver spared her a quizzical glance.

"Did she really just do that?" Lynn asked, incredulously.

"Yes she did." Diana replied, shaking her head.

"And she hasn't even had anything to drink!" Lynn commented.

"She is completely out of control!" Diana muttered.

"Might I remind you two that she is still in the cab?" Kay said over her shoulder as she rolled the window back up. "I was just letting New York know that three Montana women were in town." A few minutes later the cab pulled to a stop in front of Madison Square Garden. Kay turned to the cabbie.

"What are we doing here? You were supposed to take us to the train station!" she huffed, sounding a little panicked. He stared at her, completely speechless.

"We are right where we should be." Diana said as she exited the back seat of the cab and opened Kay's door. "Come on."

"Don't mind her, and keep the change." Lynn said to the cabbie as she handed him the fare and followed Diana out of the cab. Then she turned to Kay.

"The train station is underneath Madison Square Garden, remember?"

"No, I didn't remember – I told you I was directionally challenged." Kay muttered in embarrassment.

"Honestly, Kay, even the blind woman noticed that much!" Diana joked as they headed in to catch the train.

"Would you care to explain your 'yee-haw' moment?" Lynn asked when they were seated on the train.

"Nice, quiet women don't make history." Kay said with a grin. "We all need to remember that!"

• • •

As far as Diana was concerned, the highlight of the trip to New York was the day they toured the 9/11 Memorial, which was in the final stages of construction. While Diana had enjoyed all the sights and the plays, visiting the memorial was something she felt compelled to do. When they were planning the trip, Kay didn't really want to tour the memorial because she thought it would be depressing, and she wanted to focus only on happy things while they spent time together. Her son was appalled that she would call herself an American, be in New York, and not pay her respects with a visit to the memorial. She considered his opinion, and changed her mind. Diana considered that to be one of Kay's best qualities. She was definitely opinionated, but she kept an open mind and was always willing to listen and re-evaluate.

The new World Trade Center soared into the sky to a total height of 1776 feet. It gleamed in the morning sunlight and was visible from anywhere in the city. The memorial was designed to symbolize the loss of life as well as the physical void left by the terrorist attacks. The sites of the original twin towers were occupied by two one-acre reflecting pools. The names of the 2983 victims are inscribed on seventy-six bronze plates attached to the parapet walls that form the edges of the pool. The site designers thought of everything, even including the phrase "and her unborn child" after the names of the ten expectant mothers who died on 9/11 and the expectant mother who died in the 1993 World Trade Center bombing.

The huge waterfalls cascading down the sides of the reflecting pools muffled the noises of the city, and the contemplative nature of the memorial was further enhanced by the nearly 400 sweet gum and swamp white oak trees planted throughout the site, with special placement of the Survivor Tree, a Callery Pear, which had been recovered from the rubble at ground zero a month after the terrorist attack – and long after recovery workers expected to find anything alive there. It was nursed back to health, and then survived a second assault when a windstorm uprooted it before it was moved to the memorial site. Because of its tenacity, it has become a symbol of hope and rebirth to a great many people. As she stood in front of the pear tree, Diana remembered visiting the Oklahoma City Bombing Memorial with Gray and Riley. There had been a survivor tree there, too – an eighty year old American elm which originally provided the only shade in the downtown parking lot. That tree also became a symbol of human resilience and now holds a place of prominence in the Oklahoma City Bombing Memorial Site with the inscription,

"The spirit of this city and this nation will not be defeated; our deeply rooted faith sustains us."

To demonstrate that faith, each year volunteers plant seeds from that elm tree and return the saplings the following spring, so that on the anniversary of the bombing, those saplings can be distributed. Thousands of Survivor Elm trees now grow in public and private places all over the United States, and in the years to come, there will be thousands more.

Diana closed her eyes to absorb the ambiance and decided that both the 911 Memorial and the Oklahoma City Bombing Memorial sites had a hushed, spiritual feel to them. Given the lives sacrificed in each place, maybe they had become sacred ground.

• • •

On the night before Kay and Diana were to return home. The three were comfortably sprawled on the couch and love seat in Lynn's living room, each with a glass of wine.

"I'm glad we did this. We should plan regular get-togethers." Kay commented.

"I agree." Lynn agreed. "We had a great time, and between the two of us we kept Diana from getting lost, breaking her neck, or going into any men's restrooms." Diana raised her glass in a mock toast to the two of them and smiled without comment. Her smile faded pretty quickly at the next bit of conversation.

"I want to know more about your eye problems." Lynn said.

"Me too," Kay said. "Let's make a game out of it, okay?" Diana nodded, somewhat reluctantly. She didn't mind a general explanation, but somehow she didn't think that's what these two were after. There was a fine line between complete denial, acknowledging that she had a disability, and focusing on that disability too much.

"Share a minor annoyance." Kay said.

"Airport security." Diana said promptly. Both her friends looked surprised and a little puzzled.

"You had to go through the extra screening in Billings. Does that happen a lot?" Kay asked.

"Let's just say it happens often enough that I don't think it's random." Diana agreed.

"What do you think it is?" Lynn wanted to know.

"My stress level goes up in airports because it's hard for me to see, and they probably pick up on that." Diana explained. "So good for them that they are well trained and alert, but do I really look like a terrorist?"

"Of course you don't! But you did refuse to go through the scanner." Kay reminded her.

"Yeah, well, that's my right. I shouldn't be harassed for making that choice. I bet terrorists go through the scanner without any complaints so they won't draw attention to themselves."

"Why do you make that choice?" Kay wanted to know. "I meant to ask that before but I forgot."

"I don't buy off on the idea that those things are safe! When you get an x-ray of your teeth at the dentist's office, they put a lead apron over you and the tech steps out of the room. Think about that!" Diana said emphatically.

"I guess I never thought of it that way." Kay agreed. "I don't fly all that much, so…"

"X-rays are cumulative, or so I've read. I know they say those are low level radio waves, and not x-rays, but I'm not sure I believe them, and I'm not taking any chances." Diana said firmly. "Everything we go through for airport security, like taking off our shoes, coats, belts and jewelry, is because a terrorist already got through their security. Honestly, one time Gray had to take the Kleenex out of the pockets of his cargo shorts! So, anyway, in my opinion, what they do is spend a lot of time and money harassing ordinary people while the real terrorists get right by them."

"I think you have some valid points, but it sounds like more than a minor annoyance." Lynn commented.

"It's minor because it only upsets me when I travel." Diana retorted with a grin. "The rest of the time I don't think about it."

"Okay, share a major annoyance, then." Kay said.

"When people tell me I should just get new glasses or have Lasik surgery. That happens a lot. I mean, seriously? If it was that easy, I'd have done it years ago!"

"Do you explain?" Lynn asked, adding, "I'm just curious."

"Sometimes I explain that retinitis is all about the retina, which is on the back of the eye, but most of them don't get it. They just think if it's an eye problem, then glasses or surgery will fix it." Diana replied with a shrug.

"What do you find the most frustrating about the daily details of your eye issues," Lynn asked. "I mean, besides people who don't get it?"

"I hate being a pain in the butt to the people around me!" Diana said promptly. "I have to ask my family," she smiled ruefully and gestured to the two of them, "or my friends, to do things for me that I wish I could still do for myself." Actually, this was not quite true. It was a close second, but at the very top of her list of frustrating things associated with her failing eyesight was that she didn't feel competent to babysit her grandchildren. It bothered her so much that she had never articulated it to anyone, and didn't want to share it even with her close friends, so she had offered up another of the frustrations on her list.

"That's part of aging, though. We're all going there in some way and at some point. I mean, the body wears out, right?" Kay commented.

"Yeah," Lynn agreed. "Sad but true. My body is wearing out even as we speak; I creak when I move some days!"

"And let's not forget that our minds are wearing out too, or at least slowing down." Kay rolled her eyes. "I can't remember what I'm doing half the time."

"Okay, back on track here!" Lynn said sternly. "Name one thing you used to do just for you that you really miss."

"Sewing." Diana replied after considering for a moment. "When I stopped making my own clothes, I thought it was because I was too busy with little kids underfoot, but a few years ago when quilting got really popular, I thought I'd enjoy doing that."

"And you didn't?" Kay asked. Diana shook her head.

"Not so much! Everything about sewing frustrated me." She said. "For instance, I have trouble threading the needle on my sewing machine."

"I never thought of that!" Kay exclaimed. "How do you thread your machine?"

"I use a bright light, a magnifying glass, multiple attempts, and lots of swearing." Diana laughed. "I think it's the swearing that makes the difference!"

"So you aren't able to sew at all?" Lynn asked.

"I still do some mending. Once I get the needle threaded – either for hand sewing of machine work -- and so far I always manage to get that done -- I can patch jeans, sew on buttons, do a hem or replace a zipper – stuff like that." Diana replied. "But I don't make clothes, I don't do quilting, and I probably won't be teaching any of my granddaughters to sew either. If my eyes are this bad now, by the time the girls are old enough to want to make their own clothes…" she shrugged.

"I don't think very many girls make their own clothes these days, or do much sewing at all anymore, so that might not have worked out anyway." Kay commented and Lynn nodded in agreement.

"Hmm." Lynn replied. "I thought for sure you'd say playing the piano. I asked you once about that and you said you didn't play much anymore. Then when we were in Missoula you said you had picked it up again."

"I did stop playing for quite a few years, because it was hard to read music and learn new songs. Then when my oldest granddaughter started taking lessons, my son told her I used to play. It was fun to talk to her about her songs and sit at the piano with her. One thing led to another and I started remembering and playing some of the pieces I had memorized years ago."

"See? You can still share stuff with your grandkids!" Lynn said.

"Do you learn new songs, or just play the old ones?" Kay wanted to know.

"If I really like a song, I take the time to learn it." Diana explained. "And I still play the ones I memorized years ago." She didn't mention that sometimes she played with her eyes closed, just in case at some point she couldn't see the keyboard anymore. She figured it was best to be prepared, if possible.

"I'm glad music is back in your life." Lynn said approvingly. From there the talk turned to other hobbies, and Diana was glad to have attention shifted away from her eye issues. She was getting better about acknowledging that she had a disability, but she didn't really like talking about it in much detail.

Kay pursued artistic endeavors in phases, so she described her most recent activities of making pottery, scrapbooking, painting miniatures and taking photographs. Lynn had just started writing a book, which generated quite a bit of discussion about her characters and the details of the plot.

CHAPTER 12

More Travel

• • •

FIVE DAYS BEFORE GRAY AND Diana were to leave on a road trip, Gray added up the miles they wanted to travel, divided by the time they had available, and decided that driving was not going to be an option.

"I guess you'll have to make airline reservations." He said casually to Diana on Sunday night. She had suspected this would happen, and had suggested several times that Gray re-think his plan to drive. He had finally done as she asked, but she was not thrilled with the prospect of making last minute travel arrangements.

Monday morning found Diana in front of her computer screen muttering to herself about people who procrastinated and then delegated the crappy jobs. With a sigh, she started making arrangements for their ten day trip.

They planned to leave on Friday and fly to Seattle to visit a nephew for the weekend, then on to California to spend a few days at a resort hotel on the beach. From there they would rent a car and drive to visit more nieces and nephews before dropping the car off at the airport and flying back home. It took six hours to arrange all the flights, ground transportation and hotel reservations. Each hotel had to have an exercise room so Gray could work out, and the rental car had to be picked up in one location and dropped off in another. She printed each e-mail confirmation and put them in a folder so she'd have a hard copy of their itinerary. Midway through the list of reservations, she realized she hadn't received a confirmation for the very first flight from Great Falls to Seattle, and panic ensued when she couldn't remember what website she'd used. She ended up calling Delta Customer Service where a very helpful representative was able to track down the reservation for her and e-mail her the confirmation. The nice lady was also able to correct a typo Diana couldn't believe she had made.

"Thanks so much." Diana said, "I can't believe I typed my own name wrong!"

"No problem." The customer service representative laughed. "We've got to keep those TSA people happy. They really hate it if the reservation and the name on the photo ID don't match." With that little glitch straightened out Diana had just finished double and triple-checking everything and was relieved to be finished.

Then her cell phone chimed and she read a text message that the Alaska Air flight from Seattle to California was leaving on time – within the hour -- today. She groaned. That particular flight was supposed to be six days away, on Sunday! Once again she had to call customer service and explain her mistake so the reservation could be changed to the proper day. She used her cell phone because she had the Alaska Air customer service number programmed in there already, and was stunned when the call was dropped midway through. While she was frantically trying to call back, using her land line this time, and getting a busy signal, the nice customer service lady called her cell phone and left a voice message that the changes to her reservation had been made. The message also said that an e-mail confirmation would be forthcoming. Diana waited anxiously until finally, three hours later; the promised confirmation appeared in her in-box. She placed the printed copy in her folder, and, as she checked all the arrangements one more time, she wondered how long it would take a normal person to accomplish what it had taken her all day to finish. She was also rather curious if the arrangements she thought she made were the arrangements she actually made. Only time would tell.

• • •

Gray and Diana were spending a few days at a resort hotel on the coast of California. They enjoyed leisurely breakfasts, walks on the beach, elegant dinners overlooking the ocean, and thanks to modern technology, Gray was able to check his e-mail and stay in touch with his office every day. He was doing exactly that on the afternoon that Diana decided to spend some time at the pool.

She was a little surprised to find more than a dozen young women lounging around the pool in deck chairs. Some of them had obviously been swimming and some were just enjoying the sunshine. She surmised that their husbands were probably attending a seminar or something. Diana wanted to lie in the sun for awhile, but she didn't want to intrude on this group of women who were chatting casually.

In hindsight, Diana realized several things. It would have a good idea to stop walking while she looked for an unoccupied lounge chair. It would have been wise to remember that she had no peripheral vision. It would have been prudent to notice that the pool was the same color as the patio, making it hard to see where one ended and the other began. If she had done any one of those things, maybe she would not have walked off the edge of the patio and plummeted to the bottom of the swimming pool. As her feet hit bottom, she gave an inward groan and looked around, glad that she had not been carrying her kindle, or a towel, or her phone.

The pool was only four feet deep, and Diana was five feet four, so she didn't even get her glasses wet, but everyone was definitely staring at her as she stood there, chest-deep in the water, wearing a bathing suit that was not visible under a pair of shorts and a tank top. Trailing her hands lazily through the water at her sides as if she did this every day, she glanced around trying to get her bearings and eventually located the stairs leading out of the pool. After a moment or two, she walked leisurely towards them and up out of the water. She smiled at the women in the closest group of lounge chairs as she picked up a towel from the table and draped it casually around her neck. There were startled expressions on every face she saw. Yup, she was definitely the center of attention.

"I've always wanted to do that!" She said, with a perfectly straight face, as she walked towards a lounge chair off by itself. She adjusted her chair and made herself comfortable, reclining in the sun with her eyes closed. After a few minutes, the buzz of conversation resumed. She had no doubt that if the ladies weren't whispering about her now; they would certainly do so later. Maybe they would refer to her as a crazy woman when they told their husbands.

She stayed long enough for her clothes to dry and then went back to the room. Gray had gone to use the treadmill in the workout room, so she didn't mention her afternoon adventure to him. He found out about it eventually, of course, but it was several weeks later when he overheard her telling stories to the grandkids. They giggled when she described how she had walked right into the pool wearing her clothes.

"You didn't tell me that!" Gray exclaimed. The kids thought it was hilarious that they were the first ones to hear the story.

"Didn't you know, Grandpa?" Will asked.

"No." Gray answered, shaking his head.

"A girl has to have a few secrets, don't you think?" Diana asked and both Eliza and DeeDee grinned and nodded in agreement.

• • •

The swimming pool story was too good not to share with Kay and Lynn, so the next time they had a conference call, she told them all about it.

"That is too funny!" Lynn sputtered. "Something always happens when you go off by yourself and think you can see where you are going!"

"And you didn't tell Gray?" Kay asked when she stopped laughing.

"He's heard about or seen so many of my screw-ups that I'm sure he gets tired of it. Anyway, I knew he'd find out when I told the grand-kids." Diana replied.

"What in the world would you do without him?" Kay asked, soberly.

"Yeah," Lynn chimed in. "If something happens to him, you'd be in real trouble!"

"Everything would change, that's for sure." Diana agreed. "But that would be true of anyone who lost a spouse, right? It doesn't matter if you have a disability or not, everything changes." Diana had thought about it, and she knew Gray had too. But she refused to worry about it, so as usual, she resorted to humor.

"If something happens to him, I'll just have to get myself a seeing-eye guy." It took a minute for her friends to realize what she'd said.

"Don't you mean a Seeing Eye dog?" Kay asked.

"Dogs can't drive, silly! No, I'll get a Seeing-Eye Guy." She paused and then added, "And I'll interview him using Braille!" After a beat of silence, both her friends roared with laughter.

"Seeing-Eye Guy? That's good!" Kay chortled.

"Does he know you call him that?" Lynn wanted to know between giggles. He did actually, and some days he even found it mildly amusing.

• • •

"They don't have a reservation for us." Gray said as he came back to the pickup. "Are you sure this is the right hotel?"

"I know it is, because I used points to pay for the room." Diana said, wondering why she hadn't printed off the reservation confirmation as she usually did and stuck it in her purse. Well, she thought crossly, she had done that at least fifty times and never needed it that was why!

Naturally, the first time she needed a confirmation number would be the one time she didn't have it with her.

She sighed and wondered if maybe it was time for her to stop being the one who made reservations. Gray certainly didn't need one more thing to do, though, and making reservations and packing her own things was about all she did when they traveled. Gray had started packing his own things years ago after the trip when she forgot to pack his underwear. He did all the driving, checked in, handled their luggage and guided her through the parking lot in the dark, and then through the dimly lit hallways to their room. She had a tendency to get lost in the corridors of hotels.

Once they were in their room, he also unpacked their toiletries and lined everything up beside the sink – his things on the left and hers on the right. It wasn't that she was incapable of doing things like that, she assured herself; Gray was just thoughtful. Or perhaps he still remembered the time she had used his electric toothbrush instead of her own. They had been side by side on the counter, hers with a rubber band around the handle, put there specifically so she could differentiate hers from his.

Gray also took the wrapping off of the soap and put it into the shower along with the shampoo and conditioner, with the shampoo on the left and the conditioner on the right, just like they had it at home, and he located the hairdryer for her. She tried to remember to thank him for being so considerate, and he always laughed and said it was worth it not to listen to her fumble around huffing and puffing in frustration. Anyway, she was positive that she had made the reservation at this hotel, but she could easily have gotten the date wrong.

"Okay, well, I'll see if they have a room available then." Gray said and went back to the lobby. Luckily, there was a room available and the two of them checked in, had dinner and went to bed. When they returned home the next afternoon, the first thing Diana did was log on to her computer to check on that reservation. With a groan, she picked up the phone and called the hotel.

"Hi, this is Diana Tucker calling. My husband and I stayed at your hotel last night. I thought we had a reservation but you didn't have a record of it, so when I got home, I looked it up, and I'm embarrassed to tell you that somehow I managed to make the reservation for tonight instead of last night." The person on the other end of the phone was very helpful.

"I see. Well, that's not a problem; we can just cancel the reservation for tonight, since you've already been here." Diana could hear the smile in her voice, of course, and certainly couldn't blame her for being amused. She herself would be amused if this kind of thing wasn't becoming more the rule than the exception.

"Thanks very much." Diana said when everything was taken care of. "I won't make any promises, but next time we come to town, I'll try really hard to make the reservation for the night we actually plan to stay there."

• • •

"Today was a long day, but at least we don't have to get up so early when we go home." Cole commented. He and Beth and their two children were having dinner with Gray and Diana, all of them looking forward to spending the next few days in Disneyland.

"Oh? I thought our return flight was early too." Gray said with a glance at Diana.

"No, our return flight doesn't leave until eleven." Cole replied. Diana shrugged. She had planned to check all the return travel arrangements anyway. Once they were back in their room, she dragged out their itinerary and noted that, as Cole had said, their return flight left at eleven instead of seven in the morning. That meant that their shuttle reservation for the trip to the airport had to be changed. She called to reschedule, sharing a laugh with the customer service representative about using the wrong flight information.

"The good news," Diana told Gray, "Is that instead of leaving the hotel at three thirty in the morning, we can leave at eight thirty." And the bad news, she thought to herself, was that she spent a lot of time checking, double-checking and triple-checking everything she did because she made so many mistakes when she read things. In this case she had mistakenly used the time of the departing flight for their trip to California instead of the time of the flight back to Montana. So far, none of her mistakes had cost them any money, but probably one day they would.

• • •

Gray and Diana walked out of the restaurant after dinner. There was snow on the ground and the temperature was below freezing, so Gray had clicked the auto-start button on his key fob before he paid the bill so their pickup would warm up for a minute or two before they got in.

"I see the lights on the truck." Diana said. "I'm good." She stepped forward, forgetting about the curb and would have fallen had Gray not caught her arm.

"Are you trying to break your neck?" he asked, irritably.

"I was so focused on the truck that I forgot about the curb." Diana said, sheepishly.

"Yeah, well, save us both some grief and just hang onto my arm, will you?"

CHAPTER 13

Frustrations

• • •

DIANA REACHED FOR HER BACKPACK. She had just had her hair trimmed and was on her way to the grocery store.

"Excuse me." Diana turned inquiringly to the lady who was getting her hair done in the other chair. "I just wondered if you knew your top is on inside-out." She said, somewhat hesitantly. Diana looked down and shook her head.

"Ah, no, I didn't. Thanks for telling me." She smiled and then made a detour into the restroom to remedy the situation. This kind of thing happened to her so often that she was almost over being embarrassed about it. Almost.

• • •

Arriving home from her daily walk around town, Diana unloaded her backpack and looked down as she slipped out of her shoes.

"Oh, no!" she groaned, mentally backtracking to all the places she'd been that day; post office, office supply store, drug store and grocery store. She wondered how many people had noticed that she wore two different shoes. Well, they were both crocs, but the navy one was smooth and the black one was textured with a pattern of vents across the top. She looked at her bright pink socks, which practically glowed through those vent holes and shook her head. It was too much to hope that nobody had noticed.

• • •

"What are you looking for?" Gray asked Diana, as she stood in front of the open refrigerator.

"I can't find the catsup." She replied. He reached past her and plucked the bottle of catsup off the middle shelf. "If it had been a snake, it would have bitten me." She muttered, and then, trying to be cheerful, she added, "Thanks."

The problem with the refrigerator was that she had certain places for certain things, and if they were not where she expected to find them, well, it was hard to find them. She had to keep reminding herself that having two open bottles of catsup, or pickles, or whatever, because she hadn't been able to find the first one, wasn't a federal crime. Too many duplicates would make for a crowded refrigerator, but nobody would go to jail over it. The same thing happened with items in her cupboards, especially the pantry drawers. She looked for a new jar of peanut butter one day and couldn't find one – but there were three jars of strawberry jam.

• • •

Gray and Diana had just gotten into their pickup after eating dinner at their favorite Mexican Restaurant. As Gray drove out of the parking lot, he glanced over at her.

"Your shirt is on inside out." Diana looked down at herself, and swore softly. Abruptly, she unfastened her seat belt, reached for the hem of her knit top and pulled it up over her head. Methodically, she turned it right side out and put it back on. Then she clicked her seat belt into place and stared straight ahead through the windshield.

"I take it you are upset?" Gray ventured, mildly. Diana thought about that. Yes, she was upset. She wished she didn't periodically put her clothes on inside out. But that wasn't Gray's problem. She tried to explain.

"I realize it isn't your job to see that I'm dressed properly." Diana said. "But since you didn't notice it before we ate dinner, why did you feel obligated to mention it now when we are on our way home and nobody else will see me?"

"I figured you'd want to know." Gray said, and when Diana did not reply, he added. "I guess not."

"I would want to know before I went out in public. Now it doesn't matter." She thought this should have been obvious to anyone, but it wasn't the first time she and Gray didn't see eye to eye on something. Men and women just had different thought processes. Like the time she had put her yoga pants on inside out. They were black with flat seams and no pockets, so she told herself it was an easy mistake to make. Gray had noticed the tag on the outside of the waistband in the back. Unfortunately, he hadn't noticed until she'd been wearing them all day while they did errands and grocery shopping. She couldn't decide if she would feel better being told when she made a wardrobe mistake, or if she would rather not know.

"Well," Gray chuckled, "I'm glad we're on a back street and didn't get pulled over for that wardrobe change or whatever you call it that you did back there."

"I think it's called a temper tantrum." Diana muttered with a sigh. "Sorry."

• • •

As temper tantrums went, the incident over the inside out shirt was mild. Diana could remember a couple of epic tantrums she'd had during her PMS days. Once she had spent a lovely Mother's Day with her family.

They'd had a project going, so they spent the whole weekend working together outside. They had gone out for dinner on both Saturday and Sunday nights, attended church together, and the kids presented her with the cards and gifts they had made in school. Mark gave her a set of leather coasters he had worked on in shop class. Cole's class had compiled a recipe book and Riley's class had planted marigolds in a Styrofoam cup.

On Monday, for a reason she never had figured out, even all these years later, she suddenly felt unappreciated and unloved by her husband, and it made her furious. When Gray came home that evening after work, there was a vase of peach colored roses on the piano, alongside a box of assorted chocolates.

"What's the occasion?" he asked.

"Belated Mother's Day." Diana said curtly.

"I thought you said you had a nice Mother's Day." He protested. "We spent the weekend together and went out to dinner twice. I even got you a card!"

"Well you didn't get me flowers or candy." She said, obstinately. Gray wisely did not say any more, and it took quite awhile for either of them to see the humor in that incident. Years, in fact! Whenever it came up, as it did now and then, Gray always mentioned that the following year he remembered to send Diana a bouquet of flowers for Valentine's Day. The next day, when he arrived home from work, he noticed a heart-shaped box of chocolates - one that he hadn't purchased - on the piano. Cautiously, he asked about them, and Diana explained as if the logic should be perfectly clear to everyone with a brain.

"They were on sale for half price and they are our favorite kind, so I bought them."

• • •

"How do you want to do this?" Gray asked as he parked the pickup just down the street from the Sports Club. Colored lights twinkled from store windows, and fresh snow covered the street, but the sidewalks had been swept clean. The two of them were on their way to their company Christmas Party.

"I thought you could just leave me at a table, and come and get me for dinner." Diana replied. "That way you can move around and visit with people, and I won't have to worry about running into anyone or tripping over anything." Gray nodded.

"That should work." And it did. It worked at the Christmas party and it worked at wedding and funeral receptions, and at church coffee hours. Gray either went with her if there was a buffet line, or he brought her a plate and something to drink. Especially if there were lots of people milling around, it was just easier that way.

● ● ●

One evening, they stopped downtown for a beer after a high school basketball game. Gray led her through the crowd, and found her a seat at a table with some people that they knew. Several times throughout the evening, friends stopped by their table to chat. Towards the end of the evening, a young man appeared at their table and gave Diana a friendly hug and an enthusiastic greeting.

"I haven't seen you in ages! How are you?" Diana replied that she was fine and they chatted about the basketball game and the weather for a few minutes. She didn't recognize his voice, couldn't distinguish his facial features in the dim light, and couldn't discern any clues as to his identity from the general conversation. His wife appeared on the other side of the table and someone asked if they had found out the sex of their unborn child yet. They replied that they were planning to find out at their appointment during the coming week. On the way home, Diana asked Gray who the young man was. He was the same age as their son Riley, and had lived in their neighborhood when the kids were small, but she hadn't seen him since he got married.

"How could you chat with him when you didn't know who he was?" Gray asked in surprise.

"Oh I do that all the time!" Diana replied. "Sometimes I recognize a voice, or get a clue from the conversation, but sometimes I just have no idea who I'm talking to."

"Why don't you ask?"

"I haven't figured out a way to do that. I'm used to looking like an idiot, so I could manage that part, but I don't want to make the other person feel bad. Does it really matter if I can't put a name to the blur I see as the face? I still enjoy talking to them. And if I find out later who they were, that's a bonus."

Diana had, in fact been doing this very thing long before she knew anything about RP. She had always been amazed at the ability her friends and relatives had to recognize people they'd met once or twice. She not only had trouble putting names and faces together, she had trouble remembering faces at all. She had to be around someone several times before she could recognize them.

Their family had been in an airport once when her teenage sons thought they recognized an older gentleman who had just gotten off a plane. They discussed it, trying to come up with where they'd seen him, and after a few minutes, agreed that he had been the custodian at the school where they attended a football camp -- three years earlier! Diana hadn't known whether to be amazed or skeptical. If they were yanking her chain, they were pretty good at it, which was entirely possible. If they really had recognized that guy, after seeing him a couple of times three years ago, she was one hundred percent positive that they didn't get that ability from her!

• • •

"Hi, and welcome to Shelby!" The voice reached Diana from somewhere off to her right as she approached Albertson's supermarket. The speaker was a young man, probably somewhere between thirty and forty, though she admitted she wasn't very good about judging age. He was dressed in dark slacks with a pale blue shirt, a darker blue tie, and wire-rimmed glasses, and he strode toward her with his arm outstretched.

"Thanks." Diana said, uncertainly, as she accepted his handshake and wondered if he was selling something, or if he was a missionary of some kind.

"Did you just get off the train?" The young man asked, pleasantly.

"Uh, no." Diana chuckled. "Actually, I live here."

"Really?" He said, "In Shelby? How long have you lived here?"

"About forty years, I guess." She replied.

"Oh." The young man replied, disconcerted. "I'm Charlie Tanner, what's your name?"

"Diana Tucker."

"Any relation to Mark?"

"Mark is my son." Diana confirmed.

"Great guy! Sorry if I insulted you, I thought, you know, Amtrak just left, and with the backpack…" his voice trailed off.

"Oh, you didn't insult me." Diana assured him. "I don't see well enough to drive, so I walk around town to do my errands, and I use the backpack to carry my stuff home."

"I see." Charlie said, though it was pretty clear he didn't, really. It had been Diana's experience that most people didn't quite get the not driving part of her standard explanation. A white cane or a Seeing Eye dog they would have been able to understand, but walking around like a regular person, and claiming she couldn't see very well? That they didn't get, and she had yet to find a way to explain her vision issues in fifty words or less, so she had stopped trying.

"Well, it was nice meeting you!" And with a wave he walked away. Diana chuckled to herself as she watched him walk towards his car before she continued on her way and entered the store.

She supposed it was reasonable, given that she had a backpack and the train tracks were just across the street, that Mr. Tanner had assumed she was a weary traveler. Either that or she looked worse than she thought. Her blue jeans, tee shirt and windbreaker were clean, but she supposed her hair was windblown and as usual, she wasn't wearing any makeup. When she told this story to her grandkids, she would have to remember to suggest that he probably thought she was a homeless person in need of a free meal. She was sure they'd get a big kick out of that.

• • •

Diana chuckled as she listened to Jamie describe how her husband Mitch was driving her crazy with his efforts to help around the house while he adjusted to retirement. The two women had one of those relationships where they might not talk for several months but as soon as they said 'hello' it was as if they had just talked yesterday.

"I may never retire!" Jamie exclaimed. "If we were both at home, together all day, I might have to hurt him!" Diana chuckled because this was laughable given that Mitch was six something and Jamie was five four. Jamie was an elementary teacher and thought she would be grateful that Mitch was willing to do some of the household chores and run the errands she'd been tending to after school and on weekends.

"When I ask him to go to the grocery store, he buys all kinds of junk food I don't want in the house, and he doesn't stick to a list in the hardware store either." Jamie complained.

"I know what you mean" Diana sympathized. "I always tell people that grocery shopping with a husband is worse than shopping with a six year old because you can say 'no' to a six year old. When guys go shopping by themselves, you never know what they'll come home with." Jamie groaned in agreement.

"But he is really good at fixing things and he has a garage full of tools." Diana reminded her. "I mean, I think of myself in a book store and I have to sympathize."

"Yeah, I know." Jamie sighed. "And I do try to be understanding. But what really has me tearing my hair out is the laundry! I admit that I am picky about how the laundry is done, especially my work clothes. The other day, Mitch did a load of laundry. When I unloaded the dryer, it contained a mixture of towels, underwear, jeans and some of my work clothes, including a few things that I do not put into the dryer!"

"Oh, no!"

"Oh yes! I thought I was perfectly clear when I said that while I would be grateful if he did a load of towels or underwear or his own clothes, I did not want him to launder any of my work things."

"How did you handle that?"

"Well, I didn't go ballistic!" Jamie said. "In fact, I waited until I put everything away before I reminded him, very calmly, that he did not need to wash any of my clothes. And I even remembered to compliment him for folding the towels the way I showed him, so they fit into the drawer better."

"I'm proud of you! But I'm still trying to get a mental picture of a husband who folds clothes!" Both of them laughed and then Diana went on. "Actually, I have a similar, and at the same time totally opposite situation going on." She went on to explain that Gray was picky about his work clothes too, and he had recently purchased several pairs of slacks to wear to the office. They were washable wool, so they needed to be hung up to dry.

"He is so afraid that I might accidentally put them in the dryer that he hides them until all five pairs are ready to wash, and then he washes them and hangs them up to dry."

"Gray is doing his own laundry?" Jamie asked in amusement. "That's hard to imagine!"

"Not all his laundry, just his new pants. Mind you, I had to show him how to operate the washing machine, and buy liquid fabric softener – because all I had on hand were the softener sheets for the dryer. But otherwise, he has politely refused my help."

"But you still do the rest of the laundry, right?"

"Yeah. Last week I actually called him at work because there were two pairs of slacks in the hamper and I wanted to be sure he hadn't put his new ones in there accidentally. He said he'd worn some of his old slacks and those I was still allowed to wash and dry."

"Lucky you!" Jamie teased.

"And he always lets me know whenever he finds a stray sock that I overlooked in the hamper, or something I dropped on the floor so it didn't make it into the washing machine. It gets annoying!"

• • •

"I can't believe you are up on a ladder!" Cole scolded his mother. "What are you doing?"

"I'm cleaning out the gutters."

"Yeah, I figured that part out, but you could fall, you know."

"I'm being very careful. I hold on with both hands. I move the ladder often and make a million trips up and down instead of leaning." Cole rolled his eyes.

"And I have my cell phone in my pocket!" She pulled it out of her pocket and held it up, triumphantly.

"How does that help, exactly?" He asked with more than a hint of sarcasm.

"Well, if I do fall, and I'm still conscious, I can dial 9-1-1." Diana explained. Cole didn't think she was funny, and Diana was in complete agreement that falling off a ladder would not be a laughing matter. That was the reason she really was very careful. On the other hand, she was determined to do everything she could do as long as she could do it. She worked in the garden and did most of the yard work, including trimming bushes, raking leaves and mowing the lawn. Everything took longer because she misplaced gardening tools, and sometimes she had to go back and mow places she missed, but oh well. She enjoyed being outdoors and wasn't punching a clock.

• • •

It was the middle of the night when Diana got out of bed to make a trip to the bathroom. She moved around the edge of the bed and straight ahead keeping her right hand outstretched until she came to the wall on the far side of the room. There she turned left and trailed the fingers of her right hand lightly along the wall until she got to the doorway, where she made a right turn and walked down the hallway, again trailing the fingers of her right hand along the wall until she got to the bathroom doorway. She always made this nocturnal journey to the bathroom and back without lights, and mostly without waking up completely. For some reason, on this particular night, she got disoriented, missed the bathroom door, and tried to walk into the linen closet. That door was closed, and bumping into it made enough noise to wake Gray. He got out of bed and turned the hall light on so he could see what she was doing and she could see where she was going. She was not grateful. The glare momentarily blinded her, the fact that she had gotten lost in her own hallway was acutely embarrassing and on top of that she felt bad about waking Gray. By the time she got back into bed both she and Gray were wide awake and not speaking to each other. When she told Jamie about it over the phone, it somehow became a lot funnier than it had been in the middle of the night.

"Why don't you keep a flashlight beside the bed?" Jamie asked.

"I didn't think I needed one." Diana grumbled. "But maybe I do. I already have a flashlight in my purse and one in each of my closets! Although, with my luck, if I kept a flashlight beside the bed, I'd forget it was there, knock it over when I got out of bed and then trip over it. I can just see myself flailing around trying to catch hold of something to keep my balance, crashing into the wall and pulling down the curtains and the curtain rod."

"How do you manage when you stay in a motel?" Jamie asked when she had stopped laughing at the picture Diana described.

"Usually there's a nightlight or we leave the light on in the bathroom and close the door most of the way. But thanks for bringing that up so I have something else to look forward to! It's probably just a matter of time til I get lost in a motel room, huh?"

"We'll just hope you don't wander out into the hall!" Jamie agreed

• • •

"I wonder what's going on there." Gray commented as they pulled into town.

"What do you mean? Where?"

"Over there. At the motel." Diana turned her head to look to the right and saw an array of emergency vehicles including an ambulance, two police cars and a fire truck, all with their lights flashing.

"It doesn't look good." Diana commented.

"You didn't see all those flashing lights before I mentioned them?" Gray asked.

"No peripheral vision, remember? I just see straight ahead. I was looking down at my phone and only saw the flashing lights when I turned my head and looked right at them." Diana said.

• • •

Shopping was not quite as much fun as it had once been. Though she was not colorblind, exactly, she did have trouble differentiating between similar colors, especially navy and black or black and brown.

"May I help you?" the clerk asked.

"Could you tell me what color this is?" Diana responded, holding up a belt.

"Its black on this side," The clerk replied and then turning it over, added, "and brown on this side."

"Thanks. I'm looking for one that is black on both sides." Diana said. But she didn't end up buying a belt after all. She couldn't tell if any of the belts were the same color on both sides, and she couldn't tell which side was black and which was brown. She had marked all her dark colored pants on an inside label with laundry pen, but she couldn't see any way to mark a belt.

Sometimes Diana mistook mannequins for salespeople, or salespeople for mannequins. The first wasn't so bad, since rarely did a mannequin get upset over being asked a question. However, salespeople really did not care to have the clothes they were wearing fondled while she mused,

"I wonder if they have this in my size."

CHAPTER 14

Entertaining The Grandchildren

• • •

DIANA'S HUSBAND AND CHILDREN WERE vigilant so that Diana wouldn't trip over babies learning to crawl, toddlers learning to walk, or any of their toys. By the time the grandchildren were able to talk, they knew their grandma couldn't see very well.

• • •

"I'll take Grandma." Five year old Will announced as Mark pulled into the school parking lot. They were on their way to a school program for his sister DeeDee. Although it was afternoon, and Diana thought she could see pretty well, she dutifully took his hand as soon as they got out of the SUV. He looked up at her and grinned as they walked across the parking lot towards the school.

"If anyone sees us, they think you are holding my hand so I won't get run over." Will explained.

"But really, *you* are holding *my* hand so *I* won't get run over!" Diana agreed cheerfully. "I guess that's our private joke."

"Yup!" Will grinned. And when they got into the auditorium, Diana was glad she had a hand to hold, however small, because she couldn't see a single thing except for the lights on the stage, which did more to blind her with their glare than to illuminate her path. Will guided her down the aisle to their seats and when it was time to leave, he remembered to grab her hand.

• • •

Diana had always enjoyed shopping for her own children and thought that when she had grandchildren, she would buy things for them too. Under the circumstances, she didn't buy very much for anyone, including her grandchildren, except for birthdays and Christmas when she asked for specific lists and did her shopping on-line. Instead, she set aside a few dollars each week and contributed to their college funds. She reasoned that they wouldn't miss the clothes or toys she might have shopped for, and she hoped that someday they would be glad for the nest egg she helped create.

• • •

Diana decided to wear a dress to church since the weather was warm enough that she would probably only need a sweater to ward of the morning chill. She chose a floaty crinkled cotton maxi-dress with mauve flowers on a beige background, and slipped into her beige leather sandals. Perusing her jewelry box, she decided to go with her new pewter necklace. The clear stones seemed to pick up the color of whatever she was wearing – navy had made them look blue the last time she'd worn it. After she put it on, she asked Gray if it looked okay. He was used to that – she nearly always asked his opinion when she wore something other than jeans. He looked her up and down.

"That necklace looks green." He said. She looked in the mirror. She'd assumed the stones would pick up the mauve flowers, but maybe they had picked up the green color of the leaves in the print instead. She couldn't tell. She really liked this necklace, so she went out into the living room to get a second opinion.

"Dee, does this necklace look okay with this dress?" she asked her eight year old granddaughter. Dee looked up and immediately shook her head.

"It looks green, Grandma. You should wear your diamond necklace. And wear the earrings too." Without a word, Diana went back into her room and changed her jewelry, ignoring Gray's smirk.

• • •

Once she quit driving, it wasn't just the actual shopping that presented the problem; sometimes it was getting whatever she purchased home from the store. If it didn't fit into her backpack, she had to ask someone for a ride, or she had to get creative.

"So, do you want to hear what happened to me the other day?" Diana asked her grandkids.

"Sure!" They replied. The three of them were always up for a story from their crazy grandma, and she always exaggerated for their amusement.

"Well, I had a present to wrap..." she began.

"For my birthday!" Eight year old Will, interrupted.

"Yes. And the only wrapping paper I had was pink." Diana said.

"Yuck!" He closed his eyes and gave a dramatic shudder.

"That's what I thought too. I mean, I like pink, and the girls like pink, but I didn't think that you would like pink." Diana grinned at him.

"You were right, Grandma!" He said with an emphatic nod.

"So, what did you do?" The younger of the girls, Eliza, age five, wanted to know.

"Well, I walked to the store to buy some wrapping paper. And that's where the trouble started." The kids grinned at each other.

"The first problem was that they only had the kind of gift wrap that comes on a roll. Like Christmas paper, you know. Those rolls are about this big" She held her arms wide, and the kids nodded in understanding. "And the second problem was that I liked two different ones and I couldn't decide which one I liked better."

"Did you buy them both?" Eliza wanted to know.

"Good guess. I did buy them both." Diana nodded.

"There isn't anything funny about that story, Grams." DeeDee, the ten year old objected, rolling her eyes. She was named after her Grandma Diana, but everyone called her DeeDee or simply Dee.

"Buying the paper wasn't the funny part." Diana assured her. "The funny part was when I paid for it and left the store to walk home. I thought I would just carry a tube in each hand, because they were too tall for one of the bags that the store has. But that looked a little weird.

"Yeah, like you had a sword in each hand." Will chuckled.

"Something like that, yes. Or maybe ski poles. But right away I had a problem."

"What was it?" Eliza asked.

"I couldn't open the door to get out of the store, with both hands full. So I decided to put them both under my arm." The children looked at each other and waited for the punch line.

"I got the door open, but when I walked through, the rolls of paper bumped on the doorway and they fell on the ground." Eliza giggled.

"That isn't funny!" Diana scolded her with mock seriousness.

"Yes it is!" Eliza replied, still giggling.

"So I picked them up and decided to put them in my backpack."

"I bet that looked weird!" DeeDee rolled her eyes and shook her head.

"Probably." Diana agreed, with a grin. "The two rolls of wrapping paper stuck out the top of my backpack, one on each side of my head. I think I might have looked like a giant bug with antennae. I'm not sure, because of course…." She paused and waited.

"You couldn't see yourself." The children chorused.

"Grandma! Did anyone see you?" Eliza asked the question, but all three children waited for the answer with big grins.

"Lots of people saw me, sweetie. I don't think I've ever had that many people slow down and wave and smile when they drove by." Diana said, then put a finger to her chin and added with mock innocence,

"Or maybe they were laughing and pointing. What do you think?" All three kids dissolved into giggles.

• • •

"Grandma?" Leah was standing in front of Diana's Christmas tree.

"Hmm?"

"How come your Christmas tree doesn't have any decorations on it?"

"I was waiting for you and Erik to come and decorate it for me." Diana answered. The children were thrilled, and there followed about twenty minutes of fun as ornaments were put on the tree, all on the lower branches most easily reached by children ages five and two.

Diana loved Christmas and the whole house was decorated. There was a nativity set, a display of snowmen, Santa in a sleigh with a bag of wrapped presents, several different kinds of wreaths and an assortment of candles. It was the only time of year that there was decorative clutter in her home.

The Christmas tree was pre-lit, and Gray turned the lights on when he got up in the morning and left them on til they went to bed at night. Diana loved the tree and the lights, but she couldn't tell if it actually had decorations on it or not, and she couldn't really see to decorate it herself, so some years, it didn't get decorated.

• • •

Diana's father had been an outdoor kind of guy who went fishing and hunting. She liked fish, but she had never developed a taste for wild game, preferring her steaks, roasts, and hamburger to come from the grocery store meat department, thank you very much. Since he owned guns, Duane Williams had insisted all his daughters learn basic gun safety. Although Gray was not a hunter, he and Diana made sure their children learned about gun safety too. To them, possibly because they were born and raised in Montana, gun safety was something everyone should learn, not much different than knowing how to swim, using basic tools, driving a car, or balancing a checkbook. A life skill, in other words.

When their children were young, Gray and Diana had taken them gopher hunting. They usually went on a Saturday or Sunday afternoon, and the process included driving into the country and shooting at, but not necessarily hitting any of the pesky little critters. Although every now and then a gopher got himself killed by darting in front of a BB, for the most part the outings were about target practice and gun safety.

Will was about eight when his dad set up empty Diet Coke cans on a bench in front of a dirt embankment at their family cabin and brought out his old BB gun. While the other children bounced on the trampoline, Will practiced with the gun. Several adult family members stood chatting as they supervised both activities.

Diana was a stickler for gun safety and while watching Will, she noticed that his gun was not level and that he was jerking the trigger, so his shots were missing the cans and going into the dirt.

"Will, you need to hold your gun level and squeeze the trigger gently." He was frustrated with not hitting any of the cans on the bench, and her remark did not sit well with him. He gave her a disgusted look, stood up and thrust the BB gun towards her. She was pleased to notice that he did not point it at her or anyone else, so at least he was conscious of gun safety.

"You do it then." He said, none too politely. She hadn't expected him to do that. Although she had been a fairly decent shot when she was younger, she doubted she could hit the broad side of a barn now. She had started this exchange, though, so she decided that at least she could demonstrate the proper way to hold the gun level and how to squeeze the trigger instead of jerking it. She took the BB gun from him, set it against her shoulder, laid her cheek beside the stock and sighted down the barrel at the cans on the bench. She was right handed and used her right eye to aim. Her vision wasn't great in either eye, but her right eye was the worst of the two. Surprisingly, the cans were blurry, but she could actually see them lined up on the bench. She aimed at one of them and gently squeezed the trigger. Pop! The can fell over. Stunned and trying not to show it, she turned and casually handed the BB gun back to Will with a smile. He stood there looking first at her, then at the can now lying on its side, and then back at her.

"Grandma! You hit the can!" He exclaimed, his eyes wide with surprise.

"If you hold the gun level, get the target in your sights, then gently squeeze the trigger without jerking, you'll hit the can too." She assured him, as calmly as she could manage, because she was just as shocked as he was. Will finally took the gun from her outstretched hand, still looking dazed, and went to set the can back up. Diana turned to her son Mark and the rest of the family, all of whom were standing there staring at her in amazement. She grinned.

"Can you believe I did that?" She exclaimed, and none of them could.

• • •

It was Thanksgiving weekend and Diana was thrilled to have all her children and grandchildren in one place. The older grandchildren were outside playing in the snow, but Erik had come inside because he was cold, and Diana was keeping an eye on him. It shouldn't have been difficult; he was on the couch watching a monster truck video on an ipad and she was checking her e-mail. She heard paper rustle, looked up trying to pinpoint where the sound came from and saw the top of Erik's head, just visible above the kitchen counter.

"Hey buddy, what are you doing?" There was no answer, so she got up to investigate. Erik looked up with his cheeks bulging. She repeated her question and this time he replied.

"Habbin a nack!" He was a verbal child, and usually easy to understand, but his mouth was not just full, it was over-full. Diana glanced at the counter and saw an open bag of marshmallows.

"You decided to have marshmallows for a snack?" she asked. He nodded as he stuffed another marshmallow into his already full mouth. Diana struggled not to laugh. Honestly, if one of her own children had sneaked marshmallows right before lunch she would have marched him directly to the garbage can and insisted that he spit them out immediately. But for some reason, whenever one of her grandchildren did something a little bit naughty, she found it highly amusing. Her sons half-jokingly accused her of going soft and said she was losing it. They were probably right because she hadn't even thought to check Erik's little fists for more contraband.

"Sweetie, I don't think your parents want you eating marshmallows right before lunch." He stared at her, his big blue eyes wide with innocence, but he said not a word in reply, probably because he was still chewing.

"How many marshmallows did you have?" He shrugged.

"I don't know." He said after he swallowed, and then he crammed the marshmallow he had been clutching in his other hand into his mouth. Diana groaned, wondering what Erik's parents would say when she confessed that she had been outsmarted by their three year old!

• • •

"Where did you guys park?" Dee asked. They were sitting in the bleachers watching Will play basketball. Diana shrugged and shook her head.

"I have no idea."

"Well, did you park by the door over there" Dee motioned to the opposite side of the gym. "Or did you park in front of the school?"

"I got out of the pickup, grabbed Grandpa's arm and just went wherever he took me." Diana said.

"Oh yeah! It's dark out. I forgot!" Dee said with a grin. "I should have asked Grandpa!"

• • •

Diana smiled as she inhaled the holiday aromas of freshly baked bread and roasted turkey. She loved to cook and bake for her family, but this year the basket of dinner rolls on the kitchen table was not a product of her culinary skill. Dee had volunteered to help with Thanksgiving dinner, and she had been the one to bake the rolls and make the pie crust.

Gray carved the turkey while Diana mashed the potatoes and made gravy. As she worked, she remembered the first holiday she and her oldest granddaughter had baked together. Dee had been two when Diana let her crack the eggs and stir the filling for pumpkin pie. Dee was so excited about helping in the kitchen that the next week her mother found her standing on a chair she'd pushed up to the counter, trying to make her own breakfast.

From them on, whenever Dee came to visit, they baked something; usually cookies of some kind, but sometimes they made banana bread or huckleberry muffins. Will and Eliza often joined in the fun. Will always wanted to run the mixer. According to him, boys were really good at operating machinery. Diana used those times in the kitchen as mini math and reading lessons as they talked about fractions and the different measuring cups used for wet or dry ingredients. She always had the kids read the recipe, both for their benefit and to double check that she hadn't misread it. To keep them on their toes, sometimes she purposely misread the recipe so they could catch her mistake. When whatever they were baking was out of the oven, they had a tea party and sampled their product while they chatted.

As she got older, Dee began to do a lot of baking at home, too. At first she used mixes but soon she graduated to looking up recipes on the internet and doing most of her baking from scratch. She cried the time she tried to make frosting with granulated sugar instead of powdered sugar. Diana helped her re-read the recipe and explained the difference between the two kinds of sugar.

"All good cooks make mistakes sometimes, but I bet you'll never do that again!" Diana had assured her. When Dee was ten, Diana got her a junior cookbook for Christmas and Dee started making simple meals. Not too long after that she asked for a real cookbook like the one Diana had in her kitchen.

"When I use a recipe, I write a note beside it, Grams, just like you do in your cookbooks." Dee reported. "Then I can remember if it was good or not."

Diana taught Dee to bake bread the summer she was eleven, explaining the purpose of each ingredient – sugar to feed the yeast, salt to keep it under control, and how to make sure the temperature of the liquid was just right; warm enough for the yeast to work, but not hot enough to kill it. She demonstrated how to work the dough and explained that kneading made the bread light and chewy instead of heavy and tough. Dee read the recipe, measured all the ingredients and did all the work. Her first dinner rolls were the hit of the family reunion. With her newfound confidence, she practiced making other kinds of bread at home.

This Thanksgiving, Diana taught her to make pie crust, using the never fail recipe she'd relied on for years, and showing her the trick of rolling out the dough between pieces of waxed paper so it wouldn't stick to the counter. Her first crust had to be patched in several places, but the second one went a lot easier. Diana used that as a life lesson too and she and Dee had a nice chat about how practicing helps you get better at whatever you are trying to do. While Dee was working on the crust,

Diana supervised Eliza as she mixed up the pumpkin filling. She had beamed when Gray proclaimed it the creamiest pumpkin pie filling he'd ever eaten.

As they sat down to eat, one of the things Diana was thankful for was that she was able to pass on her love of cooking to her grandchildren.

• • •

Diana's entire family and a couple of guests were gathered for dinner, so Cole and his daughter were setting up a card table for extra seating.

"Let's move it over this way a little bit." Cole said, "So Grandma can get through here if she needs to go into the other room."

"Because Grandma is blind, right?" Leah confided in a stage whisper.

"Well, she isn't blind, but she doesn't see very well, and it is kind of dark in here." Cole replied. Leah nodded wisely. She was six and in the first grade, and she heard things, as children do. Obviously she had heard Diana joking about being blind.

• • •

"Hey!" Seven year old Eliza exclaimed as she and her siblings and Gray piled out of the pickup on their way into the grocery store. "We're in a parking lot! Who has ahold of Grandma?"

• • •

"There's a fly in here!" Eliza's eyes followed the buzzing in the window. Diana could hear the fly, but she did not see it. She and three of her grandchildren were having a tea party and had been in the middle of a discussion of DeeDee's day at school when they were interrupted by the fly in the window.

"Are you going to kill it?" Will asked.

"I guess I can try." Diana said as she got up to retrieve the fly swatter. She moved towards the window, where the buzzing had stopped.

"There he is!" Eliza shouted, pointing to the windowsill. Diana finally spotted the fly and swatted at it, but missed.

"He got away!" Will shook his head in disgust.

"He's in the window again!" Eliza called out. Diana took another futile swat at the fly and missed again. This was not going to work, she thought, so she turned to the children and put her hand to her ear.

"Do you hear that?" The children looked puzzled and all three of them shook their heads.

"I don't hear anything." Will said.

"That pesky fly is saying, 'nah, na-na, nah, nah! You can't get me!'" Diana declared in a taunting sing-song voice. The children laughed as Diana had intended, and then DeeDee took pity on her, picked up the flyswatter and smashed the fly on her first try.

When the tea party resumed, the discussion turned to all the bugs that Grandma couldn't see, and she told them about when she and Grandpa had lived in South Carolina. Grandpa kept telling her there were bugs and lizards and even snakes all over the place. But she didn't see them. The children shook their heads and grinned into their tea cups.

• • •

"Grandma? Do you have a stapler we can use?" Six year old Leah asked. She and her cousin Eliza had been busy creating art work for the past hour or so. Diana kept a box of art supplies available for them, but the stapler wasn't something they were allowed to use unsupervised.

"I think so. Let's go look." She knew she had a stapler, but the more pertinent questions were where had she put it and would she be able to find it. She was busy scanning the shelves and opening drawers, wondering if she should ask Gray for help when Leah caught up to her.

"Here it is!" Leah crowed as she plucked the stapler off the middle of the shelf where it should have been in plain sight. The familiar phrase 'if it had been a snake' slithered through her mind as she complimented Leah on her great eyesight and reminded her to have a grown-up help her use the stapler.

• • •

Diana walked towards the golf cart, but before she could slide behind the wheel, Will materialized in front of her, blocking her path.

"Where are you going?" he asked, sternly, clearly a nine year old with an agenda.

"To my house." She replied. Gray and Diana had recently purchased a small cabin about half a mile from the family vacation home. The golf cart was the only motorized vehicle Diana drove, and she only used it travel between the two places. She actually preferred to walk, but this morning she had several things to carry, so she needed to use the cart. Apparently not on Will's watch, she thought, smothering a grin.

"I'll drive, Grandma." Will said, holding his hand out for the key which she gave up without a word of complaint. He slid behind the wheel and Diana walked around to sit in the passenger seat. There were worse things than having a nine year old chauffeur, she thought. He was a better driver than she was, and she was glad he was such a considerate kid.

CHAPTER 15

Developments

• • •

"Have you noticed the vision being obscured by the cataract in your right eye?" Dr. Thomas asked.

"I have, yes. That eye is just blurry now." Diana replied, and Dr. Thomas made a note on her chart. At the conclusion of her appointment that day, he gave her the name of an eye surgeon to contact if she decided to have cataract surgery. She thought about it for several weeks and then decided that any improvement in her vision would be a good thing.

The eye surgeon, Dr. Davis, traveled all over the state, so Diana was able to have the surgery performed in Shelby and then see her local eye doctor for her after-care.

On the morning of the procedure, she reminded herself that the process was streamlined for her benefit as much as for the surgical team. With that in mind, she tried not to feel as if she were on an assembly line.

She completed her paperwork, and then she waited. There were at least a dozen other patients in the waiting room, some wearing eye patches which indicated they were already involved in the process. After awhile, she moved from the waiting room to what she privately referred to as the eye drop room. There she was asked which eye was scheduled for surgery, her chart was checked, presumably to make sure her recollection matched the written record, and when it did, they used a marker to draw an "X" on her forehead above her right eye to designate the eye scheduled for surgery. It was nice to know that checklists were in place to keep things like that straight. The five or six patients in the eye-drop room were shuffled from chair to chair in an order that indicated they were moving towards the front of the line. Each move to a different chair was accompanied by another regime of eye drops.

"Who knew one eye could accommodate so many different kinds of eye drops?" The technician quipped cheerfully, echoing Diana's thought almost exactly. Diana only heard her say it once while she waited in that room, which led her to believe that the comment was part of the pre-surgery choreography.

At last, Diana was moved to the chair with wheels and the next time she was moved, it was to be wheeled into the operating room for the actual surgery. As usual, the bright lights were painful. She steeled herself against the discomfort with a mental reminder that Dr. Davis was the one who really needed to see what he was doing, and that it wouldn't take very long. She was startled when he asked her if she was all right.

"Yes." Her voice was muffled by the sterile cloth that covered the rest of her face, including her other eye.

"You moaned." Dr. Davis said. "Are you in pain?"

"The lights hurt." She mumbled.

"Oh. Hang on, it won't be long."

"Okay." Diana was glad her eye was taped open so she didn't have to worry about blinking. Regardless of how long it felt like it was taking, she knew it only took a few minutes and then it was over and she was wheeled into the recovery room. She was moved two more times, to different examination rooms where her pressures and vision were checked by two different technicians and the surgeon before she was finally free to go, armed with several bottles of eye drops, a schedule for when to use them, and a follow-up appointment. From start to finish the process had taken four hours.

Within a week, she received a questionnaire from Dr. Davis's office asking for a critique of their process, and an invitation to contact them to set up an appointment to have her other eye done. She didn't understand this at all. She'd known about the cataract in her right eye for several years, and had been under the impression that there was some kind of criteria that needed to be met before it was ready to be removed. It needed to get to a certain size or it needed to be obscuring her vision, or something. Suddenly, the cataract in her left eye was ready, just because she'd had the right one removed? Perhaps it had something to do with the lens they implanted when they removed the cataract. Dr. Davis had told her she would still need her glasses to read, but that her distance vision in that eye would be about the same as it was in the other eye. Maybe they liked to put in both lenses at about the same time. Diana had talked to people who had both eyes done at once and all of them were quite happy with the results. Good for them, she thought, as she jotted a note to include with her completed questionnaire.

"My vision is much improved, and I am very satisfied with the surgery on my right eye." She wrote, "But I also have RP and my left eye is my 'good' eye. At this point the cataract on my left eye is still quite small, so I think I will wait awhile before I have it removed."

• • •

Dr. Rob, a friend of her son Riley, was in town for a visit. Diana rode with them to the restaurant where they met Gray for dinner. Riley took Diana's arm in the parking lot and cautioned her about a mud puddle and then the curb. When they were seated, Dr. Robb asked if she was having vision problems, and Diana explained that she had RP. As an optometrist, he was familiar with RP, and quite fascinated by the details of her rather unique case. He asked several questions including if she had glaucoma or cataracts and she said that she'd recently had a cataract removed.

"Who did your surgery?" He asked, curiously.

"Dr. Davis." Diana replied. He grinned.

"I always ask my patients if they want a touchy feely guy with a charming personality and a warm bedside manner, or the best damned surgeon in the state."

"That's what everyone says about him, that he's the best." Diana agreed.

"What did you think of him?" Dr. Robb asked.

"I liked him. I thought he was focused and efficient, but he also took the time to give me some updated information about RP." Diana said. It had been her final check-up after surgery when Dr. Davis made the unexpected comment that her mild case of RP was probably because she was a carrier of the genetic defect that causes RP.

• • •

Diana was a little irritated that she had not done any recent research on RP. She'd heard Dr. Letz say 'no cure' when she was diagnosed, and let it go at that, turning her focus to coping with her symptoms instead of trying to fix the problem. After Dr. Davis said she was probably a carrier of the genetic defect, she got on the internet to see what, if anything, was new. The number of people in the United States suffering from RP was still small – about 100,000. There was no way of knowing what percentage of those had mild symptoms like hers. She thought it would be interesting to visit with other people whose symptoms were similar to hers, to compare notes and strategies for coping.

• • •

She discovered a lot more information than had been available at the time of her diagnosis eight years previously. It was astonishing to see the amount of research that was being done. From Wikipedia and the Foundation Fighting Blindness (FFB) website, Diana learned that the photoreceptor cells in the eyes need an exact amount of specific proteins to function properly, and that the main cause of RP is the genetic variation or mutation inherited from one or both parents. The mutated genes give instructions to photoreceptor cells telling them to make either an incorrect protein, or the wrong amount of protein.

She found reports of quite a few clinical studies and clinical trials dealing with RP, and she read them all, sometimes struggling with the scientific jargon and the ambiguity of their conclusions.

Clinical trials were defined as research studies that explored whether a medical strategy, treatment, or device was safe and effective for humans. They might also show which medical approaches worked best for certain types of symptoms or groups of people.

A clinical trial was underway on an innovative gene therapy to cure a severe form of RP known as Leber Congenital Amaurosis (CLA). More than forty children and young adults who were virtually blind had some vision restored, including a nine year old boy who no longer needed his white cane.

A three year clinical study was underway with ninety participants investigating Valproic Acid, a drug already FDA-approved for seizure disorders, It showed promise for preserving vision in some types of RP.

There was a clinical trial underway in Saudi Arabia to treat Autosomal Recessive RP – which occurred when both parents carried one copy of the mutated gene, but had no symptoms themselves. Children from those parents would have a 25% chance of being affected.

Gene therapy was defined as an experimental technique using genes to treat or prevent disease. In the future these techniques might allow doctors to treat a disorder by inserting a gene into a patient's cells instead of using drugs or surgery.

Gene therapy was being developed in Switzerland to revive degenerating cones (the retinal cells that allow people to see color and fine detail) enabling them to regain their ability to respond to light and provide vision. In theory, this approach would work independently of the underlying genetic defect. The goal for this therapy was to move into a clinical trial within three years.

The Foundation Fighting Blindness (FFB) committed two million dollars to a company that recently identified three compounds that appear to boost mitochondrial function and show potential for slowing vision loss caused by a variety of retinal degenerations. The goal was to determine which one would work best and move it into a clinical trial. In most retinal degenerations, including RP and Macular Degeneration, mitochondria (the tiny organ-like structure from which every cell gets its energy) operate at a reduced capacity because of disease-related stress. Ultimately, photoreceptors, the cells in the retina that provide vision, are lost.

Research was also underway to develop a gene therapy for people affected by the Autosomal Dominant RP. In layman's terms, they were working on two types of therapy. The one-step process would simply override the bad gene with a healthy gene. The two-step process would first knock down the bad gene and then deliver a healthy gene.

• • •

There were a plethora of other research projects being pursued as well, including the use of stem cells, retinal implants, retinal transplants, and nutritional supplements. Research funded by the FFB concluded that a regimen consisting of vitamin A, the Omega-3 fatty acid DHA, and Lutein might slow the loss of vision in people with RP. Well, Diana thought, it was gratifying to hear that research had finally agreed with the anecdotal evidence that supplements can make a difference in one's health, including eyesight.

Diana would be forever grateful to Nora, who had evolved from employer to mentor to dear friend. Nora was the one who piqued her interest in supplements, including most of those listed in the research article that were specific to vision. Diana could not prove that the supplements she had taken throughout her life were instrumental in slowing the deterioration of her vision, but on the other hand, there was no proof that they hadn't. She preferred to view it as one of those times when every little bit helped.

One of the more surprising results of Diana's research was a study conducted by the University of Alicante in Spain which indicated that the cannabinoids from marijuana might slow vision loss in cases of RP.

CHAPTER 16

Not Research, Exactly

• • •

As Diana reviewed all the new research her thoughts kept circling back to the marijuana reference. She wished she could blame what she referred to as 'the great cookie caper' on something as noble as being part of a research study. No such luck, though. It had been anything but noble; a foray into insanity perhaps, an extremely poor choice certainly, maybe even outright stupidity. Or all of the above.

It had all started innocently enough when a childhood friend had contacted her. Diana thought there was something about getting older that made people want to re-visit their youth. She'd heard more than a few people around her age relate how they rekindled old friendships and how rewarding it was. Some of them even got back together with old boyfriends. Diana wasn't so sure about that, but certainly re-connecting with Lynn and Kay had added to her quality of life, so she had entertained high hopes for this reunion with Annie. They had shared good times in their pre-teen years, and she was really hoping to add another old friend back into her life.

Though Annie had been a little wild in her younger day, Diana was hoping that she had matured into an eccentric older woman by now. She imagined the two of them getting pedicures, doing some shopping and going out for lunch while catching up on old times.

It is true what they say about the best laid plans not always coming to fruition. She hadn't even recognized Annie when she got off the plane from California. Her old friend was still tall, her hair now a beautiful shade of silver instead of the ash blonde of her youth. But she shuffled along stooped over a cane and had to stop and rest several times on the way to the car. She was frail and seemed older even than one of Diana's eighty-five year old aunts.

• • •

In one of her more lighthearted moments, Annie mentioned to Diana that she was estranged from her siblings because they didn't approve of her lifestyle. She confided, with a smirk and a twinkle in her eye reminiscent of her youthful self, that she was something of a free spirit. That part Diana remembered quite clearly, although privately she thought free spirit was a rather tame description; she would have gone with 'wild child'.

On a more serious note, Diana knew Annie was recovering from a year and a half of chemotherapy and radiation for breast cancer, but she had not really been expecting to hear a detailed description of the mammogram, the biopsy, the diagnosis and the treatment – both chemotherapy and radiation. It seemed like Annie needed to talk about it, though, so Diana listened.

"There's a good chance the cancer will come back" Annie said in a flat matter of fact tone of voice. "And when it does, I'm not going through that again."

"The treatment wasn't worth it even though it killed the cancer cells, is that what you're saying?" Diana asked.

"Yeah. The treatment killed the cancer cells, at least temporarily." Annie said bitterly, "But it also ruined my life. I can't work anymore because my brain is so foggy I can't concentrate and I get tired so easily. I have pain and the doctors can't tell me why. I can't do any of the things that made my life worth living. Did you know chemotherapy rots your teeth? I lost my smile, although maybe that isn't important since I don't have much to smile about now anyway. Some days I look around and wonder why the hell I'm still here. My life is depressing."

• • •

Annie's unexpected visit coincided with a four day visit that Lynn had been planning for several weeks. Diana didn't think that would be a problem, because Lynn got along with everyone. On the second night after Lynn arrived, Diana noticed that Annie drank more than a few glasses of wine, and as they chatted after dinner, she seemed edgy.

"Are you okay, Annie?" Diana asked.

"You are aware that cancer patients use cannabis, right?" Annie asked bluntly as she finished her second beer and reached for a third. Diana said that she was.

"Well, I use it. It eases the pain the doctor doesn't know what else to do about. And it makes me feel less stressed out."

"Okay." Diana said slowly. "Whatever works for you is fine with me."

"Except I'm out." Annie replied. "And alcohol doesn't work the same way."

"You brought pot with you on the plane?" Diana asked incredulously, sitting up straighter in her chair. The movie screen in her mind was immediately filled with pictures of drug dogs and DEA agents investigating her as a person of interest because she had picked Annie up at the airport. With an effort, she jerked her attention back to Annie.

"Yeah, why not?" Annie was saying, totally unconcerned about transporting drugs across state lines, and completely unaware of the mental nightmare playing at warp speed in Diana's head. "I've been having a joint on the deck late at night to help me sleep. But I'm out, and I need some, bad! Do you know where I can get some? I have a card." Annie did look rather desperate.

"Well," Diana said, uncertainly, "I'm not sure your California card makes it legal for you to buy anything here."

"It's legal here, though – I checked. I wouldn't have come otherwise." Annie said. Diana suddenly wished that she hadn't come, and then felt guilty for her selfishness. Most of the time she believed that everything happened for a reason, but at the moment, she had no idea what possible reason there could be for this situation, or this discussion.

"I know that usage is legal here." Diana agreed, "At least it is if you have a card. But the feds came in awhile back and shut down the providers over some kind of legal technicality. I haven't followed it that closely, so I'm not sure about all the details. The way I understand it, if you have a card, you can use pot legally, but you can't buy it legally. Or maybe you can buy it legally but you can't buy it publically. I don't know. None of it really makes sense to me." She turned to Lynn and asked if she knew any more about it.

"Not really." Lynn replied. "I haven't followed it very closely either."

"I'm freaking out here. I need it bad." Annie insisted, and she grabbed another beer and went to sit outside on the deck.

"Crap!" Diana said, "Now what do I do?" Lynn drummed her fingers on the table, thinking. After a few minutes, she told Diana that one of her husband's relatives had terminal cancer many years ago and the family had decided to purchase marijuana for him because it increased his comfort level.

"But it wasn't legal!" Diana exclaimed.

"Nope."

"How come I never knew that?"

"Because none of us went around blabbing that we were illegally buying pot. We all thought it was the right thing to do for him, even though it was illegal at that time." Lynn said calmly. She looked at Diana curiously. "If you had known -- what would you have thought about it?"

"I hate questions like that," Diana sighed. "What I would have thought – or said – about it when I was in my twenties has nothing to do with what I think or say now. I was so straight laced then." Lynn raised her eyebrows and looked at her friend over the rim of her wineglass as she took a sip of merlot.

"And what exactly, has changed?" She asked, grinning.

"Fine. I'm still pretty straight laced," Diana said. "But I have learned that the spirit of the law and the letter of the law are not the always the same. I'm wondering if this is one of those times."

"You mean when the right thing to do might not be the legal thing to do?" Lynn asked.

"Yeah."

"Do you think pot would make Annie more comfortable?" Lynn asked.

"Yeah, that's obvious. With it, she was pleasant and sociable, without it, she seems edgy and miserable. I know she's been through hell with her cancer treatment, and I meant it when I said that whatever works for her is fine with me."

"Even on your deck?" Lynn raised an eyebrow.

"Yeah, even on my deck." Diana agreed, looking somewhat surprised as she heard the words come out of her mouth. "Since I haven't had chemo or radiation, I don't have a clue what she's gone through or is going through now."

"Me either." Lynn agreed soberly.

"The problem is that I have absolutely no idea how to go about getting pot for her." Lynn took the last sip of her wine and contemplated her empty glass for a moment. Then she shrugged.

"I think I just heard you say you want to help her."

"Yeah, I think I heard me say that too. But how?"

"Everybody knows somebody who uses pot – you could start there." Lynn said softly, and Diana wondered why she hadn't thought of that, because she did know someone.

CHAPTER 17

The Great Cookie Caper

• • •

DIANA CALLED THAT SOMEONE WHOM she knew the very next morning and explained her predicament. After she recited all the details of her situation with Annie, she was given an address. That afternoon she found herself ringing the doorbell in an unfamiliar part of town. The woman who admitted Diana to her kitchen looked to be in her mid-fifties, trim in blue jeans, ankle boots and a navy blue plaid flannel shirt unbuttoned over a white tank top. Her thick brown hair was tied back in a ponytail. She didn't look like a pot head, Diana thought, and then mentally chided herself for her prejudice.

This woman looked perfectly normal and seemed quite friendly as she asked Diana to repeat what their mutual friend had told her when she set up this appointment. Once again, Diana went through the explanation about Annie being a cancer survivor with a medical marijuana card from another state, who needed relief from her symptoms. When she finished the women stared at Diana for a moment as if weighing her words. Then she excused herself and left the room, returning with a baggie of what looked like dried grass clippings.

"Have you ever tried this?" she asked laying it on the counter.

"No," Diana said, nervously, shaking her head as she reached for her purse. "I have had people suggest it to me, especially recently. I understand it sometimes helps with vision issues, and I have Retinitis Pigmentosa. I've never smoked though, and I just don't see myself learning at this stage of my life." Diana felt like she was babbling. She didn't want to be rude. She really appreciated each person in this chain of events, from their mutual friend to this woman who had trusted her enough to help solve Annie's problem. But she just wanted to finish this transaction and get going. While they'd been chatting, money had changed hands, and cigarette papers had been tossed on top of the baggie. As Diana scooped up her purchases, the other woman turned, opened the refrigerator and pulled out a baggie containing two cookies.

"Try these." She said, laying them on the counter where the baggie had been. "They are pretty strong, so don't use more than a half of one at a time. See if it makes any difference with your vision problems."

"Um – thanks." Diana said with a forced smile that she hoped didn't look like a grimace. She picked up the cookies and stuck them into her pocket. "I really appreciate your help." That was the honest truth. She did really appreciate the woman's help.

• • •

"Did you get it?" Annie asked eagerly, as Diana closed the car door. Diana sagged against the seat and nodded without saying anything. Lynn put the car in gear and pulled away from the curb. As soon as they got back to the house, Annie nearly snatched the baggie from Diana's fingers, extracted a cigarette paper from the packet, expertly rolled a joint, and went outside to smoke on the deck.

Diana spent the rest of the day considering the paradox of the situation in which she found herself. She didn't have any legal right to buy pot, so the purchase was against the law, and she was pretty sure handing that baggie to Annie qualified as distributing. And yet, in these peculiar circumstances, she felt like she'd done the right thing. She definitely wasn't cut out for a life of crime though. She was exhausted from the stress.

As far as paradoxes were concerned, Diana could see another one heading her way like a run-away freight train. Annie had gone to bed, ostensibly to catch up on the sleep she'd missed, but more likely in Diana's opinion so she could enjoy the effects of another joint she'd smoked on the deck. Taking a deep breath, Diana decided to face that freight train head-on.

"Uh, Lynn?"

"Hmm?"

"You know when I was getting that stuff for Annie?"

"Yeah," Lynn replied as she finished wiping the kitchen counter, rinsed the sponge and laid it beside the sink. Diana hesitated, unable to think where to start. Lynn gave her a penetrating look, then poured them each a glass of wine and carried both glasses to the table. She took a seat and sipped while she waited. After a fortifying gulp of wine, Diana explained about the cookies and how she came to have them.

"Cool!" Lynn replied, her eyes lighting up. "Trying pot is on my bucket list. I'd like to know what all the fuss is about, and this is perfect – we don't even have to smoke!"

"I've never really cared what all the fuss was about."

"Honestly, Diana," Lynn shook her head, "Where's your spirit of adventure?"

"I don't think I have a spirit of adventure." Diana said, tiredly. "I'm dull and boring, as you very well know, or you should know that by now from all the evidence." She paused, and then muttered, "And I don't want a tattoo either."

"Everyone our age tried pot in college, except you and me and Kay because we were all such prudes! At least I'm pretty sure Kay didn't. Come to think of it, I've never asked her, but since she was pregnant or had a baby then, it's unlikely." Lynn was silent for a minute, wondering about that and then she shrugged and continued. "Did anyone ever die from smoking a little pot? No they did not! And that myth about becoming heroin addicts after smoking one joint was a load of crap too. Let's live a little. She flashed a grin. "Tomorrow!"

"Why do we have to do it tomorrow?" Diana asked.

"Because I leave the day after that, and doesn't Gray get back from his business trip?"

"Yeah."

"And we'll talk about tattoos another day!"

It was a long time before Diana went to sleep. She knew Lynn would eventually get a tattoo. She'd been thinking about it for years and had described what she wanted in great detail, several times. The last time she'd mentioned it she said she was having an artist friend do a sketch for her. Once again Diana knew she was not in step with her peers. A majority of the people she knew had at least one tattoo. Annie had several, and a couple of them were quite large; the bird of paradise took up half her leg, and there was a work in progress on her back that included a tiger. Diana sighed again. She had never asked what else was on Lynn's bucket list – after she heard about trying pot and getting a tattoo, she hadn't really wanted to know.

Diana didn't have a bucket list, mostly because the things she wanted were not exotic enough write down on a list. She wanted ordinary, everyday things like enjoying her children and grandchildren, aging gracefully, spending time with friends, and preserving her eyesight. She didn't want to sky-dive, travel to exotic places, get a tattoo -- or try marijuana.

When she had her sixtieth birthday, Diana had resolved to take time to consider new things instead of being so quick to say 'no'. She reasoned that keeping an open mind and being willing to step out of her comfort zone would keep her from becoming even more of a fuddy-duddy than she already was. Of course, she admitted (at least to herself) that she hadn't clearly defined 'open-minded' or 'comfort zone'. Still, she thought she'd been doing pretty well with her new philosophy.

She'd traveled out of the country for the first time when she went to Costa Rica to visit friends, compensating for her vision issues by requesting a wheelchair to meet each flight and help her get to the next one. She'd had to ask her seatmate to help her fill out the forms for customs, and she had lost her wallet, but it was returned intact, and as far as she knew she hadn't gone into any men's restrooms. She thought that trip qualified as a new experience well outside her comfort zone.

Then there was that helicopter ride. She hadn't ever thought about flying in a helicopter voluntarily. Maybe in a medical emergency, but not for fun. She wasn't particularly fond of flying, especially not in small planes, and quite frankly, helicopters scared the crap out of her. But apparently Gray had a bucket list, and taking a helicopter ride was on it. When he made reservations for them to go, which he did without any discussion whatsoever, most likely very aware that she would not be enthusiastic, Diana had sucked it up and gone. The helicopter was clear, which enabled one to see in all directions including down. It was disorienting and she was scared spitless, even though she had to admit that the view of Glacier Park from the air was spectacular!

She knew Lynn was going to try those cookies, and she also knew she wasn't going to let her do it alone. She fell asleep wondering why the people around her seemed to seek out and embrace adventure while she worried so much.

After lunch the next day, they left Annie watching a movie and took the path out to the gazebo where the hot tub was located, thinking that it was far enough from the house to give them some privacy. Without any ceremony at all, they split one of the cookies and each of them ate a half. It was the worst tasting cookie either of them had ever eaten; as dry and crumbly as sawdust and with hardly any flavor. They looked at each other and waited. Nothing happened. Later they would both be glad that they hadn't brought the other cookie with them, because they might have been tempted to eat more. After about fifteen minutes of not feeling any different, Lynn groaned, slipped off her lawn chair and stretched out on a towel.

"I don't feel so good."

"What's wrong?" Diana asked anxiously.

"I feel really, really drunk, and sick. It would take hours to feel this bad using alcohol."

"Huh, I haven't noticed a darned thing." Diana commented. "You need to move out of the sun. We didn't bring any sunscreen and you'll burn if you aren't careful." It took about ten minutes to convince Lynn to move the towel she was lying on into the shade, and several more minutes for her to actually accomplish the task. She moaned that everything was spinning around and she felt like throwing up. Diana couldn't figure out why Lynn was stoned and she was unaffected until she remembered that they'd had leftovers for lunch – Lynn just had a salad but Diana had skipped breakfast, so she had a small piece of salmon too. Clearly protein slowed the absorption rate of the cookie they'd shared.

"I'm a little dizzy now." Diana said, some fifteen minutes later.

"I can hear people talking – do you hear people talking? Maybe I'm hearing things."

"I can hear people talking too, so if you are hearing things, we both are."

"I think I might die." Lynn moaned.

"That would not be good. You said nobody ever died from smoking pot." Diana wondered why the idea of Lynn dying was suddenly hilarious. She giggled, and then couldn't stop giggling.

"It isn't funny. Why are you laughing? "Lynn whined. "I said nobody ever died from smoking pot, but I don't know if anyone has ever died from eating pot. Do you know anything about that?"

"Nope. Not a thing." Diana said, fighting the urge to giggle some more. "Why didn't we do some research? We always do research."

"I don't know." Lynn replied. Diana reclined on a towel and closed her eyes. The floaty feeling was not better than the uncontrollable giggling, and she was afraid she might go to sleep, so she sat up and looked around. She noticed that they were already in the sun again, and nagged Lynn to move her towel so that she was once again lying in the shade. Diana could feel herself fighting the effects of the cookie. She should have known this would happen. Sometimes she got tipsy if she indulged in a second glass of wine, but she could count on the fingers of one hand the number of times she had been drunk, and it hadn't happened since her college days. She simply didn't like feeling out of control.

"How long do you think it will take, for this stuff to be out of our system, anyway?" Diana asked, knowing it wouldn't be soon enough for her.

"I don't know. I think it takes a several weeks."

"Oh, no! What if I have to have a blood test next time I go to the doctor?"

"Don't freak out, I think you have to check for drugs in order for drugs to show up in your blood tests." Lynn said vaguely.

"Oh." Diana sighed. "Good."

"Do you know how long we've been out here?" Lynn asked.

"Since one thirty. Can you see what time it is now?"

"Its three thirty now." Lynn reported after squinting at her watch. "God! I just want this to be over."

"Yeah, me too."

"What if we can't make it back into the house? I don't want to die out here by the gazebo."

"I thought we already decided that nobody was going to die from this." Diana snapped. "I'm sure we talked about that."

"Did we? I don't know. How are we going to get back to the house?" Lynn repeated, fretfully.

"I'm trying to think about that. My mind feels all fuzzy." Diana mumbled, struggling to focus on the problem.

"Yeah, mine too." Lynn muttered. Time didn't seem to matter, so it could have been a few minutes, or it could have been an hour later when Diana came up with a solution to their dilemma.

"Okay. I have a plan." she said triumphantly.

"What."

"First we have to stand up."

"Seriously? That's your plan? We have to stand up?"

"Come on, I'm serious about this. We have to stand up."

"I think it's a stupid plan and anyway, I don't think I can make it." Lynn said peevishly. Diana wasn't sure she could make it either, but she resolved to try. It seemed to take an inordinate amount of time for her to stagger to her feet. Once she accomplished that, she stood there awhile hoping everything would stop spinning, but it didn't. With a sigh, she figured they would have to do this in spite of being dizzy.

"We have to go in before dark. We can take it in stages. Come on, Lynn, you have to get up, now." Diana reached down trying to help her friend and nearly fell over before grabbing onto a chair for stability.

"Um, can you try to stand up by yourself?" There followed what felt like an hour but might have only been several minutes of huffing and puffing before Lynn managed to pull herself to a wobbly standing position using a chair for support. She swayed back and forth, breathing as if she'd just climbed a mountain or run a marathon.

"Now what?" she panted. "Everything is spinning. I think I might throw up." Diana ignored her comments and gestured towards the house.

"Stop whining and focus! We have to get over to that tree." She said, pointing.

"How far is that?" Lynn narrowed her eyes. "It looks like a long ways."

"I don't think it's as far as it looks. When we get there, we can rest before we go to the next tree. It usually takes less than five minutes to get from here to the house, but I don't know how long it will take today." Diana said.

"Okay. Let's go." Lynn said grimly and they started off, using each other for balance and moving slowly from one tree to the next, often staggering as the ground seemed to shift under their feet. Suddenly Lynn got the giggles, and they had to stop.

"What's so funny?" Diana ground out between clenched teeth. They were between trees and she didn't want to fall.

"I was just thinking, what if someone is watching us? We must look ridiculous leaning on each other and staggering all over the place."

"Think about something else!"

"But its funny, isn't it?" Lynn persisted.

"Thank you so much!" Diana groaned. "I really needed one more thing to worry about; making a spectacle of myself in front of the neighbors is the crowning touch!" At last they reached the house, fumbled with the screen door, and went inside. Lynn clung to the banister and made her way downstairs where she sprawled on the bed. Diana moved carefully into the living room where Annie was watching a movie. Diana wondered vaguely if it was the same movie she'd been watching earlier or a different one. Annie watched a lot of movies.

"You girls have been outside all afternoon. It's five thirty." Annie said, glancing up. "I was beginning to wonder, if..." she broke off and gave Diana a closer look. "You don't look so good."

"We each ate half a cookie and now we are sick."

"Half a cookie made you sick?" Annie asked with raised eyebrows.

"I got the cookies yesterday morning – you know, when I got your, um, supplies." Diana explained. Annie looked bewildered for a moment and then her eyes lit up.

"Edibles? You didn't tell me you had edibles!" Annie exclaimed, sitting up quickly, a grin spreading across her face. "Do you have any left?"

"We split one cookie. The other one is in the frig."

"Can I have it?" Annie asked eagerly as she jumped up and hurried across the room to open the refrigerator.

"Help yourself. She said not to eat more than half…" Diana stopped talking because Annie had already removed the cookie from the baggie and popped it into her mouth all at once. Grinning from ear to ear, she crossed the room, sprawled on the couch, and closed her eyes. Diana wanted to see how an old pro handled the trip, but she really needed to lie down, so she went into her room and collapsed onto the bed.

By the next morning, Lynn had already phoned a friend who, like hoards of other baby boomers, had smoked pot in college and was sorry to hear the two of them had such a bad first experience. When she shared that information, Diana muttered under her breath.

"First experience? My first experience will definitely be my last experience." Just then, Annie came out of her room seeming none the worse for wear.

"You are both idiots!" She exclaimed. Diana and Lynn looked up in surprise as Annie continued her rant. "You have a professional pot-head with many, many years of experience right here in residence, but did you ask for my help or advice? No you did not! If I'd known what you were doing, your first trip would have been great! You two did everything wrong!"

Good to know Annie considered herself a professional, with years of experience, Diana thought. Annie was probably right – it would have been smart to avail themselves of her expertise. She and Lynn exchanged a sheepish look as they apologized. Diana thought Lynn might have been curious about what they did wrong, but she, personally, did not want to know.

• • •

It was several days later when Diana told Gray about the great cookie caper. It had never crossed her mind to keep this adventure a secret from her husband. For one thing, she didn't believe in deceit or secrets in a relationship, and for another, one of the personality traits she and Lynn shared was that neither of them had ever been able to resist the telling of a good story. And, since they had lived through it, this wasn't just a good story; it was a great story!

"The only experience I've ever had with pot, besides catching a whiff of it now and then in a crowd at college, was once when I was with some friends in their home. They rolled a joint, and asked me if I cared to join them. I said thanks, but I'd just stick to my beer. They kinda laughed and then lit up and started passing the joint around. I had no idea I'd get a contact high from just being in the same room with them. I didn't care for it at all." Gray recounted his adventure once he finally stopped laughing about hers.

"I didn't care for it either." Diana agreed. "And it didn't do a thing for my eyesight."

"Did you think it would?"

"Not really. I just wish I hadn't done it, or at least I wish I had a better excuse. I mean, seriously? Peer pressure – at my age?" She shook her head in disgust.

• • •

"Tell me how the visit went with your old friend – what is her name?" Kay demanded. The three friends were catching up on a conference call.

"Her name is Annie." Diana replied. "And do we have a story to tell you about her visit!" She and Lynn took turns explaining how they found themselves procuring, distributing and sampling pot.

"Oh! My! God!" Kay exclaimed. "You are kidding me! I've always wanted to try pot too! In fact, it's one of the things on my bucket list."

"Why am I not surprised?" Diana moaned. "Well if you've always wanted to try it, why haven't you?"

"Well, we were all too straight in high school, and then I got married and had a baby. Something about being married with a child didn't really lend itself to trying pot, you know? After that I was just busy and I never got around to it." Kay explained.

"Yeah, same with me; I never got around to it." Lynn agreed. "But everywhere I go, I meet people my age who tried it in the sixties and seventies. Some of them still use it now and then, and I wonder what I missed, don't you?"

"That's why it's on my bucket list." Kay replied, "Of course, I wouldn't feel good about doing it right now. JP's are supposed to hold themselves to a higher standard, and although a lot of them don't bother, I think it's important. When I retire, though, I have a few things I want to do, and that's one of them."

"Are you considering a tattoo as well?" Diana asked sarcastically. "Because, just for the record, I never wanted to try pot, and I don't want a tattoo, either."

"Getting a tattoo might be interesting." Kay replied. "And you've already tried pot, so quit whining, that's off the table. I'll bet if Lynn and I put our minds to it, we could talk you into a tattoo; maybe a pretty little butterfly on your derriere?"

"Oh crap! I'm sure you could!" Diana groaned. "That's the story of my life. You two come up with a reckless idea right when I'm tired of being boring, and I get sucked in!"

"Reckless? We are not reckless!" Lynn objected, laughing.

"No we are not, but let's get back to Annie's story." Kay said, laughing too. "How do you feel about the whole experience?"

"Mixed up." Diana replied, soberly. "I'm not in the habit of breaking the law. Well, other than speeding, of course. Back when I drove, I considered posted speed limits to be suggestions!"

"I still do." Lynn agreed. "But in Annie's situation, I don't see what choice we had; it would have been just plain mean to turn our backs on her problem. She was miserable!"

"You are right about that," Diana sighed. "But I'm still not sure how we got from helping Annie to eating marijuana cookies. It's like we went temporarily insane. We didn't even do any research before we ate that damned cookie."

"I know, and we usually do the research! We had our laptops right there, too. I guess I just thought that time was a factor. I was scheduled to leave, and we had the cookies, so it was a 'now or never' scenario." Lynn sighed. "I've talked to tons of people who have used it, so I didn't think it would make us sick. I'm sorry, Diana!"

"I'm not blaming you, Lynn. I could've let you try it on your own. You didn't twist my arm. I think I've spent so many years being cautious that sometimes I just need to do something crazy. Then I regret it. The thing is, everyone I've ever heard talk about pot, smoked it. We ate it. Sheesh! I wish we'd just given the cookies to Annie." Diana said.

"Oh for Pete's sake," Kay exclaimed, "Get over it! Nobody died!"

"Well, when I was so sick, I wondered if we'd gotten some bad weed, and I thought I was going to die." Lynn retorted.

"See that's one of the things I would worry about. How do you know if you are getting good weed or bad weed? By the way, Annie said it was some of the best she'd ever had – and I think she'd had plenty!" Diana commented.

"Did either of you see in the news about marijuana substitutes? They look like marijuana, but they are sold as herbal incense or potpourri, and cost a fraction of what pot costs. You aren't supposed to smoke it, but of course, some people do and they end up in emergency rooms, mentally confused, anxious, trembling, and incoherent. Some were paranoid or hallucinating, and some were barely conscious." Lynn said.

"I am so glad that we got most of those exact same symptoms from the real thing instead of some designer drug!" Diana said sarcastically.

"You should be glad." Kay responded. "The idiots who are using that fake stuff – which goes by several names including Monkey Weed,

K2 and Spice – are putting themselves at great risk. Designer drugs are created in labs from chemicals, so nobody knows what the effects are or how the body processes them. Marijuana, on the other hand, is a plant and has been around for years, so its effects have been studied and documented, and the risk is minimal."

"There you have it, the judge has spoken!" Lynn laughed.

CHAPTER 18

Prognosis

• • •

"You are rubbing your eyes." Gray said. "Maybe you shouldn't read so much."

"Maybe you shouldn't run every day." Diana snapped irritably.

"I run to stay in shape. It isn't the same thing."

"You run because you like to run, even with sore muscles, or when you are tired. You will run as long as you can. I read because I love it, and I will continue to read as long as l can, so I think it is exactly the same thing." Diana retorted. She prayed that the day never came when she couldn't read at all, and she tried not to think about the possibility too much. While she still could – she definitely would -- continue to read.

• • •

As Diana continued to research RP, she mulled over everything she read. It was all very confusing. Science had never been her thing, and Diana knew that genetics included an astronomical number of possible combinations. She didn't want to be an expert in genetics, she just wanted basic information to try and make sense of her own personal situation. She read that genetic mutations are passed from parent to offspring through just a few basic patterns.

___*Autosomal Recessive RP*___ *- when both parents have a mutated gene, typically without showing signs or symptoms of the disease. Each child born to* *these parents would have a 25% chance of being born with two normal genes, a 50% chance of being born with one normal and one abnormal gene, thereby becoming a carrier of the disease, and a 25% chance of being born with two abnormal genes and being at risk for the disease.*

The way Diana read that, even inheriting two abnormal genes only put a person "at risk" for the disease, and did not define the severity of the disease. One in four odds didn't sound too bad.

Autosomal Dominant RP *- when only one parent has a mutated gene, each child has a 50% chance of inheriting the mutated gene – and a 50% chance of not inheriting the gene.*

Fifty-fifty was an even chance, but an even chance of what, Diana wasn't sure about. Further reading indicated that this type was particularly variable, both between and within families. Some family members were affected mildly, others severely, and occasionally the gene appeared to skip a generation altogether. None of that information was very helpful.

X-linked RP *– when the mutated gene is linked to the X chromosome. Men have one X and one Y chromosome, so a man passes his Y chromosome to all his sons and his X chromosome to all his daughters. Therefore, the sons of a man with an x-linked disorder will not be affected, but all his daughters will inherit the mutated gene. Women have two X chromosomes and pass on one of them to each child. Therefore each child has a 50% chance of inheriting one copy of the mutated gene. Males who inherit the mutated gene from their mother have a fifty percent chance of vision loss. Females carry the genetic trait and experience vision loss less frequently. Sometimes daughters are affected, but have milder symptoms.*

By the time she finished reading the definition of X-linked RP, Diana's head was starting to spin. She didn't see an explanation of why male children and female children were affected differently. But if she had inherited a mutated gene from either of her parents, this scenario could fit her circumstances, especially the last line. "Sometimes daughters are affected, but have milder symptoms."

<u>Y-Linked RP</u> – *Since only males possess a Y Chromosome, only males can be affected by and pass on Y-linked disorders. All sons of a man with a Y-linked disorder will inherit the condition from their father.*

Since she didn't have a y-chromosome and her head was already drowning in facts and figures, Diana skated right over the Y-linked definition and continued reading, coming upon another golden nugget of information.

<u>Simplex</u>: *In approximately fifty percent of all cases of retinitis pigmentosa, only one person in a family is affected. In these families, the disorder is described as Simplex. It can be difficult to determine the inheritance pattern of simplex cases because affected individuals may have no affected relatives or may be unaware of other family members with the disease.*

She stared at those few sentences for several minutes, dumfounded. Seriously? Half the time, even scientists had no clue about the cause? She had been considering the idea of undergoing genetic testing, but if half the time they couldn't tell anyway, what would be the point or spending the time and the money? There was no cure, so nothing would be accomplished or changed by the knowledge of which variety of RP she had or how she inherited it. She was most interested in defining what the chances were of passing RP on, and it was pretty clear there were no cut and dried statistics on that. Which put her right back where she started, or almost.

According to her interpretation of the jargon, 'affected' referred to someone with a full-blown case of RP. Her case was odd, her symptoms were mild, and she didn't fit neatly into any of the categories she'd read about. She reviewed all the categories again and came back to X linked RP; with the tagline

"Sometimes daughters are affected, but have milder symptoms."

That description fit her to a "T" regardless of which category she fell into, especially coupled with the professional opinion from Dr. Davis that she was probably a carrier.

• • •

Diana's family tree read like a list of degenerative diseases, including Parkinson's, heart disease, cancer, blood clots, and diabetes. It was the same for Gray's family, and for virtually everyone in her circle of friends and acquaintances. All of that was out of her control, so she decided she had gone as far as she could with her research. She resolved to periodically check for new developments and get on with her life. Scientists, even after years of research, don't have all the answers, and anyone who thinks they do need only notice the way their research conclusions are worded. For every rule there is at least one exception, not to mention innumerable variables. And the worst odds she had seen in her research seemed to be fifty-fifty.

She thought about her baby sister, who at fifty-six, the same age Diana had been diagnosed with RP; learned that she had Lou Gehrig's disease (ALS). Marcy's response had been to remind her family that everybody dies, and that she just had more of an idea how and when. Then she went on with her life, spending time with her loved ones, planting seeds and tending to her beloved flowers. Thinking about Marcy's attitude reminded Diana that nobody knows what the future holds. Each individual must deal with their own unique set of circumstances. So be it.

www.ingramcontent.com/pod-product-compliance
Lightning Source LLC
Chambersburg PA
CBHW030319180626
46810CB00003B/1157